AMBER ARGYLE

OF ICE AND SNOW

FAIRY QUEENS 1

First Edition: October 2015
Library of Congress Cataloging-in-Publication Number: 2016909643

Argyle, Amber
Of Ice and Snow (Fairy Queens Series) – 2nd ed
ISBN-13: 978-0-9976390-1-8

TO RECEIVE AMBER ARGYLE'S STARTER LIBRARY FOR FREE, SIMPLY TELL HER WHERE TO SEND IT:
http://eepurl.com/l8fl1

STRONG AS STONE,
SUPPLE AS A SAPLING.
—SHYLE ADAGE

1

Pushing aside the thick brush, Otec eased into the shadows of the ancient forest. Branches scratched at him like a witch's fingernails. He tried to ignore the itch that always started under his skin when he found himself in a space that was too tight. Soon, midday had darkened to twilight under the impenetrable fortress of leaves.

"Where's the lamb, Freckles?" Otec asked his dog. "Go get her, girl."

Freckles perked her ears and sniffed the air. They hadn't gone more than a half dozen steps before she stiffened suddenly and burst forward, right on the heels of a squealing gray rabbit.

Otec shouted at her, calling her back. But Freckles was already out of sight. Even his own dog wouldn't listen to him. Grumbling under his breath, Otec continued following the spoor his sheep had left earlier that day.

Finally, he spotted an out-of-place patch of white under some brush. He knelt down and parted the angry thorns, then took hold of the lamb's neck with his shepherd's crook. She bleated pitifully and struggled weakly to get away. Her face felt feverish under Otec's palm as he held her still. "Easy now, little one."

He gently took hold of the animal's front and back legs and hoisted her over his shoulders, her wool coarse against his always-sunburned neck. And though she wasn't that heavy, the burden weighed down Otec's shoulders.

Heading back the way he'd come, Otec didn't bother to call for Freckles—she'd get bored or hungry and come along eventually. Just when he could see the way out of the forest, something warm and runny slid down the left side of his chest. He glanced down to see himself covered in sheep diarrhea.

Otec swore—he was wearing the only shirt he owned, so it wasn't like he could change. He set the lamb down and jerked his shirt off, careful not to smear any of the excrement on his face. Then he tossed the shirt into a bush. The thing was worn so thin it was nearly useless. Besides, after he spent an entire summer in the mountains, his mother always made him a new shirt.

The shadowy breeze crawled across his skin. Shivering, he took hold of his shepherd's crook and was about to pick up the lamb again when something out of place caught his eye—a splash of red in a square of sunlight. It was far enough away he could cover it with an outstretched hand.

Squinting through the tangled limbs all around him, Otec automatically quieted his steps and moved at an angle toward the strange shape and color, hoping the lamb he had left behind would remain quiet. As he came closer, the color shifted and he could make out a pair of bent legs clad in black trousers with a bright-red tunic. Strange clothing.

Otec pushed aside some brush and saw a figure bent over something. Even at fifteen strides away, he could see that the face was fine featured with deeply tanned skin, enormous brown eyes, and thick black hair.

He knew two things at once. First, this wasn't a man as he'd first suspected—but a woman wearing men's clothing and sporting hair so short it barely touched her ears. And second, she was a foreigner. What was a foreigner doing on the edge of the Shyle forest?

She was close to Otec's own age of twenty, and she was almost pretty, in a boyish sort of way. But what intrigued him most was how engrossed she was in what she was doing, the tip of her pink tongue rubbing against her bottom lip, and her brows furrowed in concentration.

That concentration stirred something inside him, an uncanny sense of familiarity. Something about the forward bend of her head, the intensity of her gaze, sparked a deep recognition. He shouldn't be watching her—should be moving the sick lamb to the village, but he couldn't seem to take his eyes away. Eager to see what she was doing, Otec moved as close as he dared, coming to the edge of the shadows and peering at her from behind a tree.

A sheet of vellum was tacked to a board on her lap. Her hands were delicate, beautiful even, as her fingers worked a bit of charcoal in what seemed a choreographed variation of long and short strokes. Bit by bit, the drawing began to take shape. It was of Otec's village, which was spread out below them. Surrounded by the crimson and gold of autumn, Shyleholm was nestled deep in the high mountain valley. This foreign woman had somehow managed to capture the feel of the centuries-old stones, cut from the mountains by glaciers, rounded and polished for decades before they were pulled from the rivers by Otec's ancestors.

She had depicted the neat, tidy fields of hay set up against the harsh winters, even managing to give a hint of the surrounding steep mountains and hills. But what she hadn't captured was the chaos of wagons and tents set up on the far side of the village. They were a little late for the autumn clan feast, but Otec couldn't imagine any other reason for them to be there.

After his five months of solitary life in the mountains, the mere thought of the mass of people set Otec's teeth on edge. Already he could hear the incessant noise of the crowd, feel the eyes of hundreds of other clanmen who, when they found out he was the clan chief's son, expected him to be the leader his oldest brother was. The warrior his second brother was. Or the trickster who was his third brother.

They learned soon enough not to expect anything at all. When Otec wasn't in the mountains, he was carving useless trinkets or playing with the little children who didn't know he was supposed to be more. To them, he was simply the man who brought them toys and tickled and chased them when no one was looking. And that was enough.

The woman's darkened hands paused. She set aside her drawing and twisted the charcoal between her fingers. Wondering why she had stopped, Otec looked past her and saw another foreigner with the same strange clothes and dark features climbing the steep hill toward her.

Just as the man crossed under a lone tree, an owl stretched out its great white wings. It was easily as long as Otec's arm. He'd never seen its like before, white with black striations. And stranger still, it seemed to be watching the girl.

Still in the shadows, the man spoke to the girl drenched in light. "Matka, what are you doing out here?" He had a strong accent, his words flat and blunt instead of the rolling cadence of native Clannish.

Matka didn't look up at the man, but Otec noticed her shoulders suddenly go stiff. "I can't—can't be around them, Jore." Her accent was milder.

Jore rubbed at his beard, which clung to his face like mold to bread. "You have to. For both our sakes."

The charcoal shattered under Matka's grip. She stared at the destruction, surprise plain on her face. "This is wrong, Jore. I can't be a part of it."

"It's too late, and we both know it." His voice had hardened—he sounded brittle, as if the merest provocation could break him.

She tossed the bits of charcoal and rose to her feet, her gaze defiant. "No. I won't—"

Jore took a final step from the shadows, his hand flashing out to strike Matka's cheek so fast Otec almost didn't believe it had happened. But it had, because she held her hand to her face, glaring fiercely at Jore.

She opened her mouth to say something, but Jore took hold of her arm. "I'm your brother—I'm trying to protect you."

All at once Otec's sluggish anger came awake like a bear startled out of a too-long hibernation. He forgot he'd been eavesdropping. Forgot these were foreigners. Forgot everything except that this man had hit her—a woman, his sister.

Otec burst into the brightness. The man saw him first, his eyes widening. Matka was already turning, her hand going to something at her side.

A mere three strides away, Otec called, "How dare—" He came up short. Jore had drawn shining twin blades, and the ease with which he held them made it clear he knew how to use them.

"Who are you, clanman? What business do you have with us?"

"You hit her!" Otec's voice rumbled from a primal anger deep inside his chest. His hands ached to strike Jore. Ached to wrestle him to the ground. But Otec held no weapon save a weathered shepherd's crook—he'd left his bow tied to Thistle's packsaddles when he'd gone in search of the lamb.

Jore surveyed Otec, his gaze pausing on his bare chest. Otec had forgotten he'd thrown his shirt away, too. "Who are you? I haven't seen you before." Jore said.

Otec raised himself to his full height, a good head and a half taller than this foreigner. "I am Otec, son of Hargar, clan chief of the Shyle."

Jore stepped back into the shadows, his swords lowering to his sides. "You do not know our customs, clanman. I am well within my rights to discipline my younger sister."

"It is you who do not know our customs," Otec said, barely restraining himself from charging again.

Jore jutted his chin toward Matka. "Come on. You've caused enough trouble for one day."

For the first time, Otec met her gaze. He saw no fear, only sorrow and pity. He wondered what reason she would have to pity him.

She turned away and followed after her brother without looking back. Feeling a gaze on him, Otec glanced up to find the strange white owl watching him with eerie yellow eyes. The bird stretched its great white wings and soared off after Matka.

The strange trio was halfway across the meadow when Freckles came panting up to Otec's side. She plopped on the cool grass, her tongue hanging out. "Didn't catch that blasted rabbit, eh?" Otec said to her, anger still burning in the muscles of his arms.

It was then that he noticed Matka had forgotten her drawing. He picked it up. He'd never seen anything so fine, since clanmen didn't waste valuable resources on something as extravagant as art.

Otec traced the lines without actually touching them. With a few strokes of charcoal, Matka had managed to capture his village—to freeze it in time. Simply by looking at her drawing, he felt he knew her. She saw details other people glossed over. She felt emotions deeply. And she saw his village as he saw it.

Otec remembered the lamb with a start and hurried back to the forest. After settling her back over his shoulders, he called out commands to Freckles, who circled the scattered sheep, gathering them together. Otec fetched his donkey, Thistle, from where he'd tied her to the trunk of a dead tree. He led her toward the paddock to the west of the clan house, where he lived with his parents, his five sisters and eight brothers, and three dozen members of their extended family.

At the thought of them all crammed into one house for another never-ending winter filled with wrestling and lessons with axes and shields, Otec had a sudden urge to command his dog to drive the sheep back into the wilderness, to live out the winter in his mountain shack or under the starry sky. But of course that was impossible. The hay would already be laid up for the coming winter. And his mother would never allow it, even if he was nearly twenty-one.

As he unlatched the gate, Otec expected someone from the house to come out and greet him, or at least for his younger cousins and siblings to help bring the sheep in. The boys and girls were always eager for the toys he carved over the summer. But no one came, so he herded the flock into the paddock by himself and tied his donkey in one of the stalls.

He went to the kitchen door, rested one hand on each side of the frame, and called inside. A thin whimpering answered from upstairs, something not unusual in a house bursting with children. Grumbling, Otec tied up his dog outside the door—dogs were strictly forbidden inside, except for after mealtime when the floor needed to be licked of crumbs and spills.

Following the sound, Otec walked through the kitchen and the great hall, then climbed the ladder to the upper level. The sound was growing louder—someone crying. He finally pushed the door open to the room his five sisters shared. Sixteen-year-old Holla was huddled on one of the two beds, her wild blond hair a matted mess. She was his favorite, if for no better reason than because she talked so much he never had to. But also because she was the kindest, most gentle person he'd ever met.

At the sight of Otec, she pushed to her feet and ran to him, then threw herself in his arms. He grunted and stumbled back, for Holla was not a waifish girl. She sobbed into his bare shoulder—luckily the side that hadn't been covered in diarrhea.

He rubbed her back. "What is it, little Holla?"

"I'm not little!" she said indignantly. Some people found her hard to understand, for she often slurred her words. Before he could apologize, she lifted her tear-stained eyes with the turned-up corners and the white stars near her irises. He always thought she had the prettiest eyes. "I can't tell."

Otec guided her onto one of the two beds and held her hand. "Remember what Mama always says—'Never keep a secret that hurts.'"

Hiccupping, Holla nodded solemnly. "I can tell you. You never talk to anyone."

He winced. Not seeming to notice, she leaned forward to whisper in his ear, "I was waiting for Matka to come back—she always has pretty drawings. But Jore told me to get away." Tears spilled from Holla's eyes again. "I froze and he called me an idiot, and . . ." She paused, her sobs coming back. "He pushed me and I fell."

The rage roared to life inside Otec. It took everything he had to shove it back into the damp dark where it came from. "Who is he? Where is he?"

Holla wiped her face. "One of the highmen from Svass-heim. They're camping out on the east side of the village."

In his mind's eye, Otec saw the dozens of tents in that direction, and he realized they were different from the clan's tents. "All highmen?" he asked. Holla nodded. "So the clan feast?"

"Cancelled."

"What are they doing here?"

She shrugged. "Hiding from the Raiders."

"Raiders! How—" Otec checked himself. Holla wouldn't know the answers—they would frighten and confuse her too much. And right now, he needed to deal with one problem at a time. "Where is the rest of the family?"

"The highmen offered to feed the villagers the midday meal to repay our kindness." Holla's eyes welled with tears again.

With a trembling hand, Otec tried to smooth her wild hair. Sweet, perceptive Holla. "I brought you something."

She sniffed. "A carving?"

He suppressed a smile that his attempts to distract her had worked so easily. "It's not quite finished yet. I want it to be perfect." She nodded as if that made sense. "If you promise to stay here, Holla, I'll give you the spiral shell I found on the mountainside."

She gave him a watery grin. "All right."

"Stay here." Otec pressed a kiss to her forehead and left the clan house at a trot.

It was ominous to see the village so empty. There were no women perched in front of a washing tub. No men chopping wood or cutting down hay in the fields behind the houses. No children tormenting whatever or whomever they could get their hands on.

Otec rounded the Bend house—second largest home after the clan house. Another enormous owl, just like the one from earlier, was perched on the roof. Otec wouldn't have paid it any mind at all, except he was surprised to see two such birds in the same day, and away from the shadows they normally dwelled in. He would have studied the bird a bit longer, but he had more pressing matters to deal with.

On the other side of the home, a crowd had gathered. Hundreds of mostly clanwomen and children intermixed with hundreds of highmen and an equal number of highwomen—all of them under thirty years old.

For once, the familiar, sick feeling he had whenever he was confronted with a crowd failed to turn his stomach. Instead, anger simmered just beneath his skin.

2

Otec pushed through the crowd, searching the faces for Jore. He was about six people in when he caught sight of Dobber, his left cheek bruised and swollen. Something in Otec tightened. Dobber's father was a mean drunk, and Otec had hoped the man would be exiled by now.

Dobber gave him a pained smile. "You're back."

"Have you seen the highman Jore?" Otec said more tersely than he should have. After all, it wasn't Dobber's fault his father was still around.

Dobber's blond hair was the color that made it look dirty even when it wasn't. "Who?"

"He has a sister named Matka."

Dobber shrugged his thin shoulders. Gritting his teeth, Otec continued plowing through the crowd. Dobber followed.

"What's going on?" Otec asked. "Holla said something about Raiders. And where did all these highmen come from?"

"There are Raiders off the coast—they haven't attacked yet, but all the men have gone to defend our lands. As for the highmen, they've been spread throughout the clans for months, working on trade agreements. They couldn't leave by ship with the

10

Raiders out there, so High Chief Burdin sent them here for the time being."

"There's a war brewing, and no one bothered to come get me?" Otec asked through clenched teeth. "And why didn't you go with them?"

Halting, Dobber stuffed his hands in the pockets of his trousers, which were even more ratty and threadbare than Otec's. "I can handle him. My little brothers can't."

Otec had tried to make this right before he'd left five months ago. Clearly he'd failed. And now he'd insulted Dobber, but before he could think of what to say, Otec caught sight of Jore.

The rage roared from the darkness. Otec found himself running, then slamming Jore into the dirt. He threw a hard punch into the man's face and cocked back his arm to hit him again, but Jore twisted and wrapped his legs around Otec.

Otec powered out of the hold. The two men ended up rolling, and rocks and hay stubble tore into Otec's bare torso. He threw another punch into Jore's stomach and head-butted his face.

Then strong arms locked around Otec's middle and wrenched him back. "Stop it! What are you doing?" It was Dobber.

A highman stepped in front of Jore and reached out a hand. "You're done."

Unable to break free, Otec swore at Jore, calling him the vilest name he could think of.

"No need for such language." The voice rang with anger. Otec's mother, Alfhild, pushed through the crowd, her gaze furious. She stopped short at the sight of him. "By the Balance, what's going on?"

Otec tasted something metallic in his mouth and realized his teeth had cut the inside of his cheek. He spit blood into the dirt. "Jore slapped his sister. Drew his swords on me. And then he called Holla an idiot and shoved her to the ground."

Alfhild's face went white. "Jore?"

He looked at her with the one eye that hadn't already swelled shut. "I am well within my rights to discipline my younger sibling. As for the idiot . . ."

Otec's vision narrowed until he could only see Jore. With a roar, Otec broke free of Dobber. He slammed into Jore and managed to get in a couple more punches before Dobber hauled him back again, this time with help from a couple of highmen. Two more restrained Jore.

Otec struggled, angry that Dobber wouldn't let him go. Matka stepped between him and Jore. She had both hands on Jore's chest as she shouted, "Stop it!"

He jerked his head in Otec's direction. "He attacked me!"

"After you insulted and threatened his sister," she shot back.

Jore's glare moved to Matka, and he muttered something about killing idiots as babies. Otec struggled to break free again.

Matka opened her mouth as if to say something, but another man had appeared. This one was slightly older, easily the oldest highman there. "Jore, by your oaths, you will stand down."

Jore tightened his jaw and stopped trying to fight his way free of the men holding him. "Yes, Tyleze," he ground out.

Otec's vision slowly widened until he realized the clanwomen were shooing children away and backing toward the village, their gazes steely. And then Otec heard a sound he was very familiar with—the sound of Holla crying. He turned to find his sister sobbing quietly in the arms of Aunt Enrid, who lived with them in the clan house. A herd of women surrounded his sister, shushing her and patting her back. Holla loved everyone, equally and without restraint, so the clan loved her back. By the look of horror on his sister's face, she'd seen the violence Otec had caused.

All at once, the fight drained out of him. He realized Dobber was holding him tight enough to leave bruises. Scraping up

his self-control, Otec nodded for Dobber to release him, which
he did—slowly.

Otec gestured for Holla to come to him. But she shook her
head and buried her face into Enrid's chest.

Alfhild's eyes locked on Jore, and Otec actually felt sorry
for the foreigner for the briefest moment. "Is this how highmen
act when visiting lands not their own?" she asked. She stepped
up right in front of Jore, her wild blond hair only partially tamed
by a braid. "She is my daughter, highman. How dare you speak
to her thus. How dare you lay a hand on her."

He bowed. "I am truly sorry, Clan Mistress."

Alfhild slowly shook her head. "Not to me. To her." She
stepped aside, motioning to Holla, who still clung to Enrid, her
body trembling.

Jore hesitated before inclining his head a fraction. "I am
sorry."

He didn't sound sorry. Or not nearly sorry enough. As far as
Otec was concerned, Jore should be on his knees begging. But
Holla nodded. She was much more forgiving than Otec would
ever be.

Mother's glare transferred to Tyleze. "Are all your grown
men as impulsive as little children? Because I discipline little
children." The threat was obvious. If Tyleze didn't punish Jore,
Alfhild would.

Tyleze nodded toward Jore. "Go to your tent. I'll deal with
you later." Jore worked his jaw before turning on his heel and
storming out of sight.

"I assume we won't be seeing more of him?" Alfhild said it
like a question, but it wasn't. Before Tyleze could reply, Alfhild
motioned to the people around her. "The food is ready, so eat it.
And then go home."

As she turned toward Holla, her expression softened. "My
girl . . ."

But Holla shook her head, backing away from all of them before whirling around and then stumbling towards the clan house. Otec nearly went after her, but his mother grasped his arm and warned, "Not yet."

He shot a glare at Jore's retreating back, but instead his gaze snagged on Matka, who watched him with a calculating expression.

Otec's mother turned her attention to him. "What happened to your shirt?"

"A lamb was sick all over me."

"Well, that explains the smell. Come on, let's get you cleaned up." She took hold of his elbow and started hauling him toward the clan house. "Have you grown some more?" she asked loudly as she squeezed the muscles in his arm. "You're nearly twenty-one! You can't still be growing. The clothes I've sewn for you will never fit."

People were watching them. Otec waited for the familiar sickness in his stomach, but he was too tired and too worried about Holla. In fact, he hadn't felt nervous at all when he'd charged into the crowd earlier. "Mother, why didn't anyone come fetch me to fight with the men?"

She wouldn't look at him. "I've already sent my three older sons off to war."

And obviously, Otec had nothing vital to offer, or his father would have insisted.

"They've made no move to invade," his mother answered with a reassuring pat on his arm—she must have mistaken his irritated silence for worry. "And if they do, the clanmen will deal with them in short order."

Word of Otec's arrival must have spread, for as they approached the clan house, his younger siblings and cousins started coming at him from all sides, surrounding him like a pack of eager puppies, and more were coming. Unlike their adult counterparts, the children never brought about the sick feeling in his stomach.

His two youngest brothers, Wesson and Aldi, latched onto his legs and sat on his feet. One of the boys was far heavier than the other, so Otec ended up dragging his left leg behind him like a cripple. "Did you make us anything, Otec? Did you?"

He shot his mother a look, pleading for her to save him from the dozens of children, but she only laughed.

"Yes, yes," he said as he tried in vain to extricate himself. "They're in Thistle's packsaddles. I tied her up in the barn—bring her here." The children ran off. "Let the older ones get her. She bites!" he called after them.

They returned with his indignant donkey, but even she was helpless against the children's enthusiasm. Otec went to the pack saddle and began passing out some of his carvings, along with several pretty rocks and petrified shells he'd found.

Gifts in hand, his younger siblings and cousins all started clamoring for stories. But his mother shooed them away to fetch water for his bath and do several other chores, including caring for Thistle.

Before his younger brothers could lead the donkey away, Otec removed the vellum on which Matka had drawn. Immediately he felt what she'd managed to capture—permanence and age and comfort.

"Matka drew that. Where did you get it?" his mother asked from over his shoulder.

Otec untacked the corners, rolled the vellum, and tucked it into his pocket. "She left it behind when Jore hit her. I'll give it to her later."

Alfhild nodded and turned back toward the clan house. Otec hesitated, then followed her, saying, "I saw Dobber's bruises. His father—"

"His father won't be happy until everyone he loves is as miserable as he is." Alfhild frowned. "I did what you asked—

offered to banish him, split up the children among the clanwomen willing to take them. Dobber's mother begged me not to." Otec's mother gave him a sideways glance. "I know Dobber is your friend. I'm sorry."

Otec didn't want to admit he wasn't that fond of Dobber but the other man didn't have anyone else. He rubbed the back of his neck, eager to change the subject. "One of the lambs is sick, Mother."

She sent a cousin of his to fetch Aunt Enrid and headed inside.

As soon as Otec entered the kitchen, his oldest sister hugged the breath right out of his shirtless body. He gaped at her enormous pregnant belly, which pressed up against him. "When did that happen?"

Storm obviously hadn't gotten married while he was away, since she was still living with the family. She blushed the same way he did, the tips of her ears going pink before her neck turned red. "Never you mind."

Otec cleared his throat. "Well, how is the wee one?" He didn't ask who the father was. Knowing his sister, she probably wasn't certain.

"Kicks as hard as Thistle," Storm said with a smile. She clipped a few blankets around the fireplace and the beaten copper tub his other two sisters, Eira and Magnhild, had set up while his mother stoked the fire and set the iron trivet over the coals.

"It's her bite you have to watch out for." Otec rubbed his bruised shoulder. "Why haven't you kicked the highmen out yet?"

"They're not all so bad," his mother answered.

"She's being kind," Storm told him under her breath. "They're all intolerable."

Mother shot Storm a look but didn't reprimand her. "I like Matka—she's a student of herbs." His mother's voice betrayed her excitement. "She has come to study our lore. Plans to write a book on healing."

Otec told her how he had found Matka and how Jore had threatened and hit her, but Otec didn't admit to his mother that he had been watching Matka.

His mother sighed. "I wish there was something I could do about it, but she's not clannish. And with all the men gone, I can't enforce any threats."

Otec looked between his mother and Storm. "Is it really such a good idea to have five hundred foreigners in the Shyle?"

Storm ground the flour with more force than was necessary. "Aren't we lucky?"

His mother shrugged. "Half of them are women."

Otec looked out the open door, in the direction Holla had gone.

"Not yet," his mother answered his unasked question.

Old aunt Enrid stepped into the house and wrapped her arm around Otec's waist, giving him a sideways hug. "One of the lambs is sick?"

He kissed the top of her gray head. "Drenched the whole left side of my chest. He's pretty weak."

"I'll get some peppermint and chamomile down him," she said, lifting the trapdoor to go down to the cellar.

His mother set a chair for Otec outside and went about attacking his hair and beard with a pair of sheep shears. Then he took his bath in the copper tub, which was so small his knees were pressed against his chest.

His mother found him some of his father's old pants and took them in at the waist—they weren't in much better shape than the ones Otec was wearing, but at least his ankles didn't show.

One of his aunts gave him a hug and set about herding as many of his younger family members into the tub as she could find while it was set up.

While Storm let out the hem of one of his father's old shirts, Otec sat at the table, the sound of his mother's knife slicing through a potato as familiar to him as the sound of his own breathing.

His aunt started taking down the blankets—apparently she'd deemed the water dirtier than the children. A pair of his older cousins carried the tub out, and someone called, "May I come in?"

Otec shot looks of surprise at his family; visitors never asked to come in. But no one else seemed to notice.

"Yes," his mother answered.

He was even more surprised when Matka stepped inside the room. She didn't look furious or full of pity or calculating like the last couple times he'd seen her. Instead, she looked relieved. He couldn't figure her out.

His gaze wandered over her pants, which showed off her thin but strong-looking legs. Maybe women should wear pants more often. At the thought, Otec felt the tips of his ears turn pink.

Without preamble, Matka sat down opposite him, beside his mother. Otec had the impression this wasn't the first time she'd sat at this table.

"Do you not own a shirt?" Matka asked.

His neck flared red. So he wouldn't have to look at her, he took a slice of soft sheep cheese and laid it over some of his mother's thick-sliced bread.

His sister held up the shirt she was sewing. "Working on it," she shot back with a glare at Matka.

"Do you always answer for him?" Matka said. The two women locked gazes, but Storm looked away first, mumbling something about the highwoman being high and mighty.

Matka responded in clipped Svass, then took a deep breath. "I have been granted permission from my fellow highmen to go into the mountains in search of a very rare plant that is sacred to my people."

"How could a highwoman know the plants of the Shyle Mountains?" Storm growled.

Matka turned to her with an unreadable expression. "I have ways."

Alfhild gave Storm a warning look and then said, "Otec knows the mountains better than anyone else in the village."

Feeling Matka's eyes on him, Otec stared at the grain in the table. He knew if he did speak, something ridiculous would come out of his mouth, so he kept it shut.

"Specifically," Matka went on, holding a piece of rolled vellum in front of his nose, "a flower that grows in the waterfalls beneath the glacier. I need to find it before the snows come."

Still not looking at her, Otec opened the small roll of vellum to see a hand-drawn, delicate flower—it looked like some kind of lily.

"There are three petals and three sepals," Matka said eagerly, her charcoal-stained finger pointing out each feature as she spoke. "The center of each petal is ringed with yellow and burgundy. Have you seen it?"

Otec sat back, considering. She was waiting for him to speak, and this time no one else could respond for him. He cleared his throat. "There is something like that, but I couldn't say whether it is this exact flower."

She snatched the vellum back and tucked it into a pocket in her tunic. "I must see it for myself. You will take me."

He lifted an eyebrow. "It's not even in bloom."

Matka waved his words away like a buzzing fly. "I can tell by the foliage."

Otec took a deep breath, shocked to discover he wanted to say yes—that he wanted to know this woman who saw the world in such infinitesimal detail. "No," he said, hating the word even as it formed in his mouth. But he couldn't leave his family when there were Raiders prowling on the clan lands' doorstep.

His sister bit off her thread and then smirked as she handed him the shirt. He stood to put it on and caught Matka staring at his stomach just before he pulled the shirt over his head.

"I can pay you for your services, of course," she declared.

That made Otec pause. His dream was to own land at the base of the mountains. Perhaps have a family of his own. With the wages he collected from his parents, he would be in his thirties before he could purchase the land, in his forties before he'd built up a decent-sized flock. "How much?"

Matka made a dismissive gesture. "Surely a few coppers would cover it."

This time, he met her gaze and didn't look away. "Are you trying to insult me?" Angry, he started away.

Otec was at the door when she called, "Three silvers."

He paused and glanced back at her. "When?"

"Tomorrow." She was studying her fingernails as if it didn't matter whether or not he agreed. But the way her hands trembled told him it did matter. It mattered very much.

He sighed. Why were people always playing games? Why not just say what she wanted? "I can't," he said. "My family might need me."

"Oh, go," his mother said as she stood up to dump the potatoes in the cookpot. "Whatever's happening with the Raiders won't be over in four days. And we're safe here."

"Your brother will allow you to go, will he?" Otec said darkly.

He felt Matka's gaze on him as she replied, "It was his idea."

Otec stared at the floor in front of Matka's feet and realized he'd already been left behind. The Raiders were weeks away, and he would return long before anything could happen.

"I'll take you, but not your brother," he told Matka. "In four days, one of us would end up dead."

Matka hesitated. "He's staying behind."

Otec gave a curt nod and stepped into the sunshine, determined to find one wild-haired sister.

3

Otec crossed the meadow of close-cropped, dying grass dotted with haystacks. The air smelled of hay and the spice of decaying leaves. The days were growing short, so it would be night soon. He climbed over a fence and then wandered up a steep hill, scattering a herd of shaggy cattle.

He was just starting to grow nervous when he spotted Holla sitting by a little brook. She had her chin on her hands as she watched several snails inch across the surface of a white boulder in front of her.

"Why am I different?" she asked once he had climbed down to sit beside her.

Otec rubbed the back of his neck. "Everyone's different, Holla. Sometimes those differences are just more visible."

"Why does Jore hate me?"

"Because he's ignorant."

She wiped her nose. "A few weeks ago, someone called me ugly." Otec tensed, not sure what to say. Her perceptive eyes seemed to peer inside him. "Everyone says I look like you, but no one seems to mind that you're not pretty."

It was true. He wasn't considered handsome, but it had never really bothered him. "They mind that I'm awkward and shy," he said. Holla shot him a puzzled look, so he added, "Men are supposed to be strong."

That seemed to puzzle her further. "But you are strong."

Throwing his hands in the air, Otec gave up trying to explain something that didn't make sense anyway. "Just stay away from people who hurt you."

Holla nodded in agreement. "And if you can't, then kick them in the shins." She grinned and let out a wild laugh. "Lok taught me that."

Otec tried not to chuckle and ended up snorting instead. His sister laughed harder, obviously pleased with herself. He tugged on one of her braids, glad she could still smile.

He saw a block of wood and his fingers began to itch, so he snatched it up and sat on the cool grass. His knife peeled back the layers of wood one curl at a time. The uneven block quickly became an amorphous shape. Then the form began to appear, emerging from the wood as if by magic.

He took a deep breath, hesitant to tell Holla something that would upset her. "Matka wants me to take her into the mountains."

Holla frowned and prodded the wandering snails back into alignment. "You just got back."

With the smell of the fresh-cut wood strong in his nostrils, Otec used the tip of his knife to form the beaver's beady eyes, the clawed fingers, the sharp, rodent-like teeth. Steadily, Otec added chips to the delicate whorls piled around him.

"I'm better in the mountains, Holla. I don't like it when people look at me. I can't talk around them."

Holla picked up a slender stick and started snapping it into even segments. "You talk to me."

He carved while he waited for her to sort out her thoughts. Holla wrapped the broken segments, held together by the bark, around her finger. "You don't mind when I look at you," she said.

Instead of answering, Otec changed the subject. "Maybe Dobber could come over for dinner."

Her nose wrinkled. "He smells funny."

Chuckling, Otec handed her the finished carving. Her eyes lit up and she carefully tucked the beaver into her pocket. Then she turned away, squinting at the darkening sky. "Oh! Mother says I have to be home before the sun goes down." Abandoning her snails, Holla ran away without looking back.

Before dawn the next morning, Otec stepped outside, his breath a cloud in front of him. In the distance, he could see Matka waiting for him at the other side of the village, wearing the winter gear he'd sent to her, and carrying the bedroll on her back. In addition, she had slung a large satchel over one shoulder. He was surprised to also see two swords across her back. Unlike an axe and shield, swords took a great deal of training. Plus they were prohibitively expensive, which meant she probably knew how to use them.

Otec hurried toward her, only taking a dozen or so steps before the door to the clan house burst open. Holla hurtled out, still wearing only her thin underdress, her long blond hair streaming behind her. "You didn't say goodbye!" She came to a stop just before him, her face red. Otec held out his arms to her, but she hesitated, obviously hurt that he would leave again so soon.

"I'll be back before you know it. I promise."

Holla tipped her head to the side. "Sometimes you have to lose a sheep in order to save the herd. That's what Father always says." It was a saying the Shyle often used when faced with two impossible choices. She wrinkled her nose. "Does that have something to do with why you're leaving?"

Otec nodded. Holla stepped forward, touched her warm hands into his cold cheeks, and looked into his eyes. "You're scared," she whispered.

He tried to laugh it off. "I've been in the mountains all my life. They don't frighten me."

She didn't smile as she stared past him. "Matka is scared too." He turned to glance at the highwoman, who was watching them from a distance. "She has bad dreams," Holla added.

"How do you know?"

Holla didn't respond, but her eyes darted up and Otec saw the same strange owl from yesterday. Perched on the barn, it seemed to watch Matka with its eerie yellow eyes.

Otec let out a long breath. "I'll look out for Matka, all right?"

"I know. Clanmen always look after the womenfolk," Holla said in a deep voice, trying to imitate their father, then laughed at her own joke.

Otec leaned down and kissed his sister's forehead, then sent her inside. He crossed the village, heading for Matka without looking at her. She fell in beside him, effortlessly matching his longer strides. He eyed her feet. "Go back to my mother and ask her to get you some warmer boots. Those are too thin."

Matka lifted her chin. "These boots are made by some of the finest cobblers in the world. They keep my steps silent, yet I don't feel the rocks."

They'd drawn even with the tangle of tents at the outskirts of the village. Otec stopped. "They're not warm enough. I'll wait here." No need for another teary farewell.

Muttering under her breath, Matka spun around and headed back. A moment later, Jore slipped into view, the bruise around his eye an ugly purple. Otec tensed, not sure why the highman had waited for him.

"I'm truly sorry about your sister," Jore said in a low voice.

Of all the scenarios Otec could have envisioned, this wasn't one of them.

Jore turned and took a step away, but then paused and said over his shoulder, "Remember this moment, clanman."

Otec narrowed his gaze. "Why?"

Jore's eyes swept across the sleepy village, his expression sad. "Just remember." Then he slipped out of sight.

Frowning, Otec pivoted with the intent of going after Jore to ask what he meant, but Matka jogged up behind him and said, "Let's go."

He glanced at the well-used but serviceable boots on her feet. He thought they might be his younger brother's.

"Which way?" Matka asked.

Otec pointed midway up the taller mountain that flanked the pass to the clan lands. They had taken no more than a few steps out of the village when a shadow passed overhead. He glanced up to see the enormous owl fly overhead and quickly move out of sight. Otec shuddered, his skin feeling itchy.

O tec was keenly aware of Matka walking beside him.
The way she moved with purpose. The way her gaze
lingered on her surroundings, as if she had to absorb
every detail before she could look away. But she didn't seem
aware of him at all, which bothered him. And it bothered him
that it bothered him.

"Just ask," she said, startling him out of his thoughts.

He rubbed the back of his neck. Maybe she hadn't been as
oblivious as he'd thought. "Ask what?"

She tipped her head back, staring at the watery blue sky.
"What Jore and I were fighting about—it doesn't matter anymore."

"It matters that he hit you."

She let out a long breath. "Why do you care?"

"Because it's wrong." The grass ahead shifted. Relieved to
have something to focus on, Otec pulled out his bow and took
three arrows in his hand.

Matka lifted an eyebrow. "There are many, many wrongs in
the world, Otec. You can't right all of them."

The rabbit finally hopped out from the grass and looked at them, its nose quivering. Otec drew and released within the same breath, his second arrow ready to fly if the first missed. It didn't.

He put away his unused arrows. "But you can try to right the ones directly in front of you." He trotted to the rabbit, took out his knife, and killed it cleanly, then began dressing it.

Matka watched, arms folded. "That's a very simplistic approach."

Otec wiped blood from his hands onto the grass and looked up at her. She stared up at the bursts of orange, yellow, and crimson splashed across the mountainside. "Something in particular bothering you?" he asked.

She turned away. "Doesn't matter anymore. He promised."

Otec raised an eyebrow, then tied the rabbit to the back of his bedroll and they started out again.

"Did you take my drawing?" Matka asked.

His ears went red again and he didn't answer, didn't tell her that it was in his pocket even now.

"I went back for it later that night, but it was gone. You were the only one there."

"Why would I take your drawing?" he said tightly.

"So you did take it." She huffed as if pleased with herself. "Why?"

It wasn't so much the drawing as the person who drew it—a woman who realized the world wasn't a bunch of big shapes, but very fine details stacked upon each other to form a whole. It was the details that mattered, the details that breathed life into art.

Otec wanted to show her one of his carvings, to get her opinion. But his skills were rudimentary at best. He didn't have the tools he needed to make something truly remarkable.

"Very well, clanman. Keep your secrets. But when we return, I'd like it back."

"Why? You can always make more."

She didn't answer at first. "That one was special. I wanted something that could make me feel this place after I left. Do you understand?"

When Otec didn't answer, she grunted. "No. You wouldn't."

He stiffened, stung by her rebuke. Not wanting to talk anymore, he started climbing the mountain before they even reached the best spot. They were both too out of breath to speak much after that.

Just before nightfall, Otec found the cave—really more of an indentation a half dozen arm-lengths deep. He'd slept here before, had made the fire ring of stones. "We'll sleep in the cave."

Matka eyed the small space with a raised eyebrow. "I'll take my chances out in the open."

He pulled the bundle of shredded tree bark from his bedroll and fluffed the fibers. Then he struck flint to striker until the welcoming smell of a campfire filled his nostrils. He fed the little flames gently. "I wouldn't recommend it. There're bears and wolves in these mountains."

She folded her arms across her chest. "I can handle myself."

Otec put a few larger sticks on the fire. "The wolves and bears don't know that."

Her gaze narrowed. "Are you trying to seduce me?"

A laugh burst out. "Why? Is it working?" The moment the words left his mouth, horror washed through him. But Matka only chuckled.

The fire was going pretty well now. Otec set up a spit, and while the rabbit roasted, he divided the bread, cheese, and carrots his sisters had packed for them.

He glanced over at Matka to see her folding fibrous squares of paper into a shape that resembled a goat, with little triangle folds for the horns. He squinted through the smoke and thought he saw words written in a strange script across the surface.

Whispering a prayer he couldn't make out the words to, Matka set the goat on fire, holding it in her hands until the embers nearly touched her fingertips. Then she released it into the fire, closed her eyes, and leaned forward to breathe in the smoke, which suddenly smelled sweet and musky.

Otec watched her, entranced and a little uneasy. "What was that?"

She sat back, a smile touching the corners of her mouth. "A prayer of thanks to the Goddess."

"Goddess? I thought you highmen followed the Balance, as we do." To his people, the goddesses and their fairies were merely stories for children.

"Even the Goddess is subject to the Balance." When Matka dropped her head, the firelight darkened the hollows of her face, giving her statement an aura of foreboding.

Otec shivered. "Which goddess—summer or winter?"

Matka didn't answer for a moment. "Both."

He glanced up at a flurry of wings to find the owl landing in a tree not far from them. Its gaze flew to Matka.

Her face instantly went blank. After that, Otec gave up trying to get her to talk. They shared a silent meal as the sun went down and the temperature plummeted. They hadn't gone very far up the mountain yet, but already he could see his breath. It wouldn't be long before snow fell, trapping the entire village.

After showing Matka how to lay out the furs, hide side out to keep her warm and dry, Otec curled up and immediately fell asleep.

He awoke with a start sometime in the night, automatically reaching for his bow. One of the lambs was crying out in fear. Otec was cursing Thistle for not warning him and had come halfway out of his blankets when he realized it wasn't a lamb. Matka was crying out. He froze, not sure what to do. She was speaking in Svass. He didn't understand the words, yet he couldn't miss the pain beneath them.

Wearing only his wool socks, he crossed the cold ground to kneel next to her. She was tossing and turning, her short hair sticking up at crazy angles. He gently rested his hand on her shoulders and shook her. "Matka, wake up."

Her eyes flew open and she threw a punch. Otec managed to turn aside to avoid the worst of it, but he knew he'd wear the mark of it on his cheek. Her eyes cleared and a look of accusation crossed her face. "What are you doing?"

He rubbed his jaw. She knew how to hit. "You were having a nightmare."

Her gaze strayed to the tree where the owl still watched her. Matka immediately looked away, clearly terrified of the creature.

"This is ridiculous," Otec muttered. And it could be dealt with easily enough. Before he could change his mind, he grabbed his bow and strung it.

Matka kicked off her furs and started toward him. "No, don't!"

Ignoring her, he nocked an arrow and released. The owl dropped, landing with a solid thud. Its wings beat uselessly against the ground before it grew still.

Matka swayed on her feet. "You should not have done that." She turned to look at him, genuine anger in her gaze. "You've drawn their attention!"

Otec tossed his bow down. "Whose attention? It was just an owl."

She glanced at the carcass and her eyes seemed to close involuntarily, a look of relief washing over her.

"You could just say thank you," Otec growled, then fed some more wood to the fire. His gaze passed over Matka—she was still staring at the carcass, her body tense.

He sighed. "When we were little, my mother would tell us to say aloud what we wanted to dream about. It worked, some of the time. At least, my nightmares went away."

For the first time, Matka seemed to soften a fraction. "Holla said the same thing." She studied Otec warily. "You're a lot like her, you know." Coming from her, it sounded more like an accusation than a compliment.

He and his sister certainly looked alike, but then all his family had wild blond hair and pale features. "She never stops talking," he said, shaking his head. "I try my best never to get started." He picked sticks and pieces of leaves out of his socks.

Matka studied him. "No, not in that way. Obviously, neither of you have any patience for injustice. But it's more than that. It's like you're . . . innocent. Like the world has never shown you its darkness."

He tossed in another log, pretending he didn't understand. "It's dark now."

"It's like you think this is what life is. These mountains, this valley, these people. That family loves you and home is a safe place." Her voice sounded void of any feeling, but Otec knew better.

"It wasn't for you?" he asked, unable to imagine anything different.

Matka sighed, and it was as if her prickly exterior hardened back up. "This place—it is sharp and soft, the kind that takes your breath away and lets you close your eyes without fear. Where I'm from, there is only sharpness, the kind that cuts deep.

"There are things you don't know, clanman," she went on. "And those things could get you killed. I won't deny I'm glad she is dead, but she will be back. And it will be worse—for both of us."

"What does that mean?" Otec glanced at the dead owl again—Matka already believed in fairies, so perhaps she was the superstitious sort.

"Next time, don't help me." Matka rolled over and pulled the furs over her head. She murmured in a language he could not understand, and he imagined she was asking for dreams.

5

Otec let Matka sleep in the next morning. He figured she probably hadn't had much rest the night before—he certainly hadn't, not after that bit with the owl. Instead, he'd found a block of wood and begun carving.

As soon as it was light, he'd taken the owl's carcass and buried it, then set a heavy rock on top of the loose soil. Just in case.

By the time Matka finally stirred, Otec tucked the half-finished carving out of sight and handed her a breakfast of bread with ham, sheep cheese, and raspberry jam.

She sat up, rubbing her eyes, and asked brusquely, "Why didn't you wake me?"

"Because you need your rest if we're going to make it to the waterfall today." Otec set about eating.

"Where is it?" Fear tinged her voice as she stared at the spot where the owl had died.

"I buried it."

Seeming relieved, Matka started stretching her muscles. Her face was overtaken with endearing little winces as her joints popped and cracked. Wishing he hadn't noticed, Otec finished eating and began packing up their camp. Matka clumsily tried to roll up her own furs. He knelt next to her and showed her how to disperse the a flint and striker, packets of food, a small axe, extra socks, as well as some personal items so they didn't create a pocket and slip out later. He tied off the ends so nothing fell out and helped her settle the roll on her shoulders so it wouldn't pinch or rub her raw. She watched him like he was a strange creature she couldn't figure out.

Otec felt her eyes on him as he started up the mountain, noting landmarks as he went. He naturally fell into his rhythm—breathe in, wind blows, breathe out, steps fall. Listen, watch, learn. But he couldn't forget Matka and her watching eyes.

They reached the sheer cliff face. "I'll go first then toss the rope back down to you," Otec said. "Settle the loop around your chest and tighten it up."

Folding her arms, Matka turned toward him. "I insist we go around."

He raised an eyebrow. "No matter which way we go, there's a cliff involved. This is the easiest one to manage."

"Well, figure something else out."

Otec might have become angry with her, but he noticed the trembling in her hands. She must be afraid of heights like he was afraid of crowds. He looked into her eyes. "I won't let you fall."

"Do you swear it?" Matka asked softly, her eyes cast down as if she were ashamed, which he thought silly. Everyone had fears. It was how you dealt with them that mattered.

"Yes, I do."

She let out a long sigh. "All right."

He fitted his fingers in a crevice in the rock and started making his way up. The fear, the danger—it made him feel alive. Like more than just a shepherd. More than just one of twelve children in an overflowing house. Here, he was finally free.

Only when he reached the top did he allow himself to look down. Matka stared up at him, her short black hair falling across her eyes. He gave her a reassuring smile she probably couldn't make out and tied the rope securely around a tree. He tossed it down to her, somewhat dismayed when it only fell about three-quarters of the way.

Matka folded her arms around her rather sparse bosom and glared up at him. "What am I supposed to do now?"

He cupped his hands around his mouth and hollered, "Go get it."

"You promised me!"

Trying not to let his frustration get the best of him, he rubbed his forehead. "How is it you can use swords but can't climb five lengths to a bit of rope?"

"What?" she shouted.

"Matka, this is the only way up the mountain. If you've changed your mind, we can always return to the Shyle."

She paced back and forth a few times, mumbling things to herself he couldn't make out. Finally, she started climbing up the cliff face, moving faster than he thought prudent, but he dared not comment and distract her.

When she finally reached the rope, Otec let out the breath he'd been holding. "Now what?" she called, her voice shaking.

"Put the loop over your head and under your arms."

"But then I'll have to let go!" She looked down, and her tan skin lost its richness.

"Don't look down," Otec said belatedly. She buried her face in the mountain. He lay on his stomach, his face peeking over the side. "Matka." She didn't move. "Matka, look at me. Let me help you through this."

When he'd finally decided she was stuck and he would have to go down and get her, she finally glanced up at him. "You have to stop thinking about what can go wrong and focus on what will go right."

She wet her lips. "I'm not sure how."

"What do you want, Matka?"

She blinked up at him, seeming at a loss for words.

35

"Focus on what you want and don't look back."

She stared at him, her gaze hardening with determination. He nodded encouragingly. "Set your feet, release your weakest hand, grip the rope, and put your arm and head through it."

Fixating on the rope, she did as he asked. "I've got it."

"Good. Now, I'm going to stand and help pull you up, but you've still got to climb." He stood, wrapped the rope around his middle, and started pulling.

"Wait! Wait!" He peered over the edge to see Matka hanging onto the cliff with all her strength. "I'm not ready," she called to him.

Otec set his jaw, considering what to do. He could try pulling her up on his own, but where the cliff and rope met, there would be a lot of friction. If the rope broke, she would fall to her death.

"I think . . . I think I'm stuck," her thin voice carried up to him.

He found a bit of an outcropping and braced himself on it. "Matka." She didn't move. "Matka, look at me. What's the worst that could happen?"

She was trembling. "I could die."

Otec shook his head. "No. I have the rope. If you fall, I'll catch you. Don't you trust me?"

"I hardly know you," she reminded him.

"Remember what I said, Matka?" She took a deep breath and looked up at him. "Where do you want to go?"

"Up," she said so softly he could barely hear her. He nodded encouragingly. "Focus on that. Trust me. Trust yourself."

She took a deep breath and let it out slowly. Otec waited for what felt like forever, forcing himself to remain silent and not push her. Finally, she started climbing. He watched her, keeping the rope taunt. Several times she had to stop, shake out her arms, and calm her breathing.

Finally, when Matka was close enough, he reached down and clasped her outstretched hand. Bracing himself against the rocky cliff, he hauled her the rest of the way up. She landed on top of him and quickly rolled off, but he felt the impression of her body—solid and strong, much stronger than she thought she was.

She lay beside Otec, their shoulders touching and their breaths coming in ragged gasps. "I did it," she finally managed, and a grin spread across her face.

She closed her eyes, and he took the opportunity to study her. She was so different than the girls of the clan lands. Her dark lashes spread along the tops of her cheeks like the feathers of a raven's wings. And with the dappled light filtering through the trees, he realized her hair wasn't black as he'd first supposed, but a very dark brown. Matka was pretty, he realized—not classically so, but then he wasn't considered particularly handsome, either.

"Otec, why are you being kind?" she asked, still not opening her eyes. "You gain nothing by it."

"You're not used to kindness, are you?"

"Not without a reason," she said after a pause.

Otec couldn't imagine what kind of life she'd had, to make her so suspicious. "My people speak of the Balance. Like what you mentioned last night—there is light and dark in the world. Mother always says to stay as far into the light as we can manage."

"That's strange," Matka said, "since the clan lands are under the Goddess of Winter's domain, and her side of the Balance is darkness."

"Which only means we have to strive harder to stay in the light."

Her eyes opened and she turned to him. For a moment, Otec was lost in the dark depths of her gaze. She cleared her throat uncomfortably and sat up, some fir needles in her hair. Still a little lost in her, he reached up and pulled them out. She started and turned toward him as if to bat his hand away, but then seemed to relax.

Though short, her hair was so soft. "Got it," he said, his voice husky.

Matka stood suddenly and brushed the dust off her clothes, then worked at the knot still binding the rope to her chest. "How much farther?"

Otec forced himself to look away. What was he doing? She was a Highwoman, leaving in just three days. "Before nightfall." He untied the rope from the tree with vigor and was grateful when she managed to untie the rope at her chest.

Keeping far back, she peered over the edge. "Um . . . how are we going to get back down?"

"Down is always easier than up." He stepped around her and headed up the mountain at an angle. "If we move fast, we'll make it before nightfall."

Otec knew the waterfall was close when the vegetation began to change. Ferns trimmed in autumn gold and russet crammed themselves between the roots of the massive trees. Moss clung to every tree and rock. The air turned heavy and smelled of minerals.

Finally, he and Matka crossed the swift-running river and walked alongside it. More than once, Otec stopped to help her over a slippery spot or up a short cliff blocking their way. It was slow going, as she insisted on stopping to inspect and gather leaves. At one point, she sat down and hugged her knees to her chest, wonder on her face.

Otec glanced back to see the valley spread out before them—sharp hills that jutted up against rugged mountains blanketed in primeval forest. Eventually that forest was eaten up by glaciers and gray rock.

Realizing Matka was itching to draw the scene, he said, "The view is better by the waterfall." She grudgingly moved on.

Eventually, they could see the waterfall, plunging down into a rocky pool. The river widened as they approached the small, deep pool at the base, the water so clear they could see every detail of the mossy rocks at the bottom.

Otec found his favorite spot between a pair of larch trees. The ground felt soft and springy with a thick layer of larch needles, and the trees themselves would be a good wind block. He cleared the ground so he could start a fire, then looked up to find Matka already surrounded by a variety of plants. She was busily sketching each one in minute detail.

"Can you find me the plant with the flower you were telling me about?" she asked.

"I think so."

She didn't seem to hear Otec's reply as her charcoal-darkened fingers flew over the vellum. He watched her, feeling a kinship with another person who transformed something mundane into something beautiful.

After setting up the kindling for the fire, he went to the waterfall and found the plant. He brought it back for Matka, who took it eagerly and flipped the leaves over in her hands. She broke the stem with a pop, sniffing the juices. Then she licked them. Her face fell. "This isn't it."

Otec shifted from one foot to another. "I'm sorry we didn't find the plant you wanted."

She took a deep breath and let it out slowly as a smile turned up the corners of her mouth. "Let's just say I'm not as eager as my . . . employer. I have many more samples to take back with me. I haven't seen any of these in the lowlands."

He couldn't believe how changed this girl was from a couple of days ago. She just needed to get away from Jore and that eerie owl. Otec headed out to lay his snares in front of a few promising-looking warrens.

When he came back, Matka was surrounded by parchment held down by rocks. On each piece were two sketches, one of the overall plant, another a highly detailed version of the leaves. In between these sketches were bundles of leaves held together with a bit of twine. But she wasn't looking at any of them. Her gaze shifted between the verdant valley bedecked in crimson and yellow, the white-capped purple mountains in the distance, and the vellum upon which she was sketching them.

Otec stepped closer to her, careful not to disturb her drawings.

"Do you see it?" she asked softly. "The way the setting sun and the dark mountain create a jagged line of shadow and light. The way the light streams into the valley in wide beams. When I first started drawing, there was so much color I could see its opposite any time I closed my eyes. But then those colors—emerald, crimson, purple, yellow—all of them shift to black as the shadows grow deeper."

At the longing and sadness in her voice, Otec realized his mother was right. There was something soft beneath Matka's hard exterior. He crouched beside her. "What is it?"

She stayed quiet for several seconds, and he thought she wouldn't tell him. That her hard shell would spring back up, blocking her off as surely as if she'd erected walls around herself. But then her shoulders sagged. "I do not want to go back."

He carefully moved a few of her drawings, marveling at how real she'd made them look. "Back to Svassheim?" He figured the less he said, the more she might.

"Back home."

Needing something to do with his hands, Otec took out the small piece of wood he'd been working on and began carving. "Neither do I."

Matka gave a little gasp. "What? Why wouldn't you want to be among the Shyle? They are the most generous people I have ever met."

He wished he hadn't said anything. "The clans place value on women who create life and the men who protect it. And my family is the best of all of them. The strongest, the fastest, the brightest." He sighed. "And then there's me."

She seemed to consider that for a moment. "You're wrong." She let out a long breath. "All my life, I've been taught that my

41

people are better, stronger, faster. And that gave us the right to take from others, to force them to become like us."

Otec frowned. He hadn't known the highmen were like that.

"But I have spent two years among . . . different people. And they are not crude and ignorant." Matka dropped her voice. "And neither are you."

"I guess you don't have to."

She met his gaze. "Have to what?"

He shrugged. "I mean, no one is forcing you to go home. You speak Clannish remarkably well. Send Jore back with your notes, and let someone else finish the book. Stay here." Otec's voice rose with conviction. He liked the idea of her staying—this woman who was so strong, and yet so broken.

"It's not that easy," she replied, staring at one of her drawings.

"Why?"

She pursed her lips. "There are things you don't know, Otec."

Matka must have some kind of past, he decided. He'd finished carving the shape; now it was time to add the details. "Mother would let you stay. You could have a life here. But whether you want it bad enough to sacrifice whatever it is that's holding you back, that's your choice."

He turned to find Matka watching him carving with a burning intensity in her gaze. "What are you doing?"

His ears flared red again. He hadn't wanted her to see, not yet. "It's nothing."

But her quick fingers snatched the carving from his hand. She gasped softly. "It's the elice blossom." She turned it over in her hands. "You even got the square stem right!"

"It's not finished yet," Otec mumbled.

It was as if she hadn't heard him. "The proportions are perfect. And it's so delicate. When did you start this?"

His heart warmed with pride. "Yesterday."

"But you only saw my drawing once."

"I notice details. Always have." He reached into his pocket and took out her drawing of Shyleholm, sorry it was a little crumpled. He held toward her out without meeting her gaze. "I shouldn't have taken it."

She grasped it without touching him. "You can look upon your home every day. Why take this?"

"Because in every stroke and smudge, you were there." He forced himself to meet her gaze.

She watched him, her expression open and intense. A profound longing swept over her face. She glanced at his lips. That was all it took. He cradled her soft cheek in his hand, a little embarrassed because of his rough skin. And before he could talk himself out of it, he pressed his mouth to hers. Her lips were warm and full, and to his surprise, she kissed him back, taking his face in her hands. His fingers combed through her dark hair. She shuddered and pulled back, confusion warring with something else in her dark eyes.

"You don't know me," she said.

Why was she hurting so much, and who had hurt her? Otec felt a protectiveness well up inside him. He would help her if he could. "What are you running from, Matka?"

Her breath hitched in her throat and she spoke so softly he could barely hear. "No matter how fast or how far, it follows me."

He remembered what Holla had said, about the darkness shadowing Matka. "What does?"

Pursing her lips, she shook her head. "I can't."

Yes, she definitely had a past, he thought. "Where you're going is more important than where you've been."

Matka blinked at him and said wistfully, "Are you sure about that?"

Otec didn't understand how someone could be so many op-posing things without it tearing her up from the inside out. Per-haps it was. "I'm sure."

"Otec," a voice said softly. He sniffed and rolled over, hoping whoever it was would go away. But a hand shook his arm. "The light is about to hit it—you have to see." He sat up, blinking sleep from his eyes.

Matka sat near him. She was wrapped up in her furs and crouched protectively over her vellum as her charcoal scratched across the board. She kept glancing at the waterfall in the predawn light, passion enveloping her face as snow dusted her hair.

Otec immediately panicked. Getting caught in a snowstorm this high in the mountains was dangerous. He glanced up to gauge how bad the storm might be, but the sky was clear.

Sitting up straighter let the cold into the pocket of air he'd created in his furs. He shivered and turned toward the waterfall. It wasn't snowing. The mist from the waterfall was freezing in the air, stacking on the ground in delicate flakes like pressed flowers. The sunlight shifted down the mountain, lighting the sky with a thousand sparks before touching the waterfall, turning it a pale pink. The trees and ground glittered as though they were covered by diamond dust.

Frost grew slantways out of the ground like jagged, geometric leaves. Otec actually tried to pick up a piece the size of his palm, but it shattered in his grip.

"All my life and all my travels, I've never seen anything as beautiful as this," Matka said. She turned toward him. "I wish I could capture the way it makes me feel so I could look at it and feel this again."

The frost glimmered in her hair, and her cheeks were flushed with cold. Otec realized he wanted to capture the moment as well—but not the waterfall or the diamond frost. He would capture her wonder and excitement. He reached out to touch the shape of her face, letting his fingers memorize the hollows and planes. "Stay, and I'll bring you back every year."

She really smiled then. And without the hard mask she wore, she was beautiful. "I think—I think I will." She turned to look out over the valley. "If your mother . . ." she trailed off, her voice going hoarse, "Otec."

"Hmm?" he said, wondering if she'd allow him to kiss her again.

"Otec!" And this time, he heard an undercurrent of fear. Instinctively, he grabbed his bow, looking around for bears or wolves. "What?"

But Matka only pointed to the valley, her face filled with horror. He followed her gesture and didn't understand what he was seeing at first. It seemed the stars had fallen from the sky to land on his village, still in the shadow cast by the far mountains. But then Otec stood and saw, and his world crashed down upon him. Shyleholm was burning. Not just a single house and barn, but dozens.

"What?" he managed dumbly.

"No. This cannot be." Matka scrambled to her pack and pulled a contraption out of a case. It was a cylinder that lengthened when she pulled on it. She peered through it and her grip tightened. "The village has been attacked."

"What?" Otec couldn't seem to get his mind to work properly. It was like a gear that kept missing the cog.

Fists clenched at her sides, Matka stared up at the sky. "So many betrayals." She turned back to him. Gone was the vulnerable girl. This woman wore the face of a warrior, and he realized he did not know her at all. "Otec, your village has been attacked by Idarans."

"Raiders," he gasped. But it couldn't be Raiders—they couldn't have made it this far inland.

"Yes, Raiders," Matka responded, anger building in her voice.

His breathing came fast and shallow. "How could you know that?"

"I saw it in the telescope."

He snatched the telescope from her grip. "No! It's probably just a barn that's caught a couple of houses on fire." Even as he said it, he knew it wasn't true.

He peered through the telescope. Everything appeared closer. It took him a minute to find his village, but when he did, his breath caught. Buildings were burning. His villagers were running. Screaming. Dying. But by the Balance, some were fighting, too.

"Hurry, Otec. We must go for help," Matka said from where she knelt, packing her bedroll. His brain finally woke up. He realized all the men in the village—the protectors—were gone. His brothers and sisters were alone down there. And his mother. And his aunts and uncles and cousins. And his friends.

He rushed to his pack and shoved everything inside. "You're going to have to keep up. I can't slow down for you."

"How far to the nearest village?"

Otec ignored her question. "If we hurry, we can reach Shyleholm by midday."

He swung his bedroll over his shoulder, took his bow in his free hand, and started off at a jog. Matka was right behind him.

"Shyleholm . . . Otec, you can't go there. It's already lost. You have to reach the next village and rouse your clanmen."

He didn't bother to slow. "My family isn't in Argonholm."

She snatched his arm. "If you go down there, you'll die with them."

He whirled, jerking his arm free, and barely stopped himself from shoving her. "They are not dead," he said, his voice hard. "Don't you dare say they are dead."

"No, I didn't—"

He turned and broke into a full-on run, not caring if she kept up or not. He didn't stop until he reached the cliff.

Matka came panting up as he secured the rope around a tree. "Listen to me, Otec. If you want to help your family, you need allies. You can't just go barreling into the midst of the Idaran army. The Raiders take slaves. You'll need help to free them."

She had a point. "After I'm down, pull the rope up and come down yourself," he said. "You go on to Argonholm. Tell them what you saw." He tied the rope around his chest and started down.

"I don't know the way," Matka yelled from above him.

"Head southwest!" he shouted back at her.

"Even if I don't get lost, it will take me twice as long without a guide," she called once he'd reached the bottom and was busily untying the rope from his chest. "Otec, going for help is the best chance you'll have at saving them!"

He paused, actually letting her words sink in. And he knew she was right. He was too late to stop what was happening—by now, it was already over. He thought of Holla, her hands on his face. His mother, watching him leave. The weight of his two brothers as they wrapped around his legs. The rest of his sisters. Storm, pregnant. By the Balance, they could already be dead.

When Matka stepped down beside him, he was crouched low, the heels of his hands pressed into his eyes in a useless attempt to block out the images of his family running and screaming for their lives. He couldn't help them. Couldn't do one thing to stop it.

Matka rested a firm hand on his shoulder. "Otec?" But he could barely breathe from the horror rolling through him. "Otec, where do you want to go?" He looked up sharply, prepared to snap at her for throwing his words back in his face, but her expression wasn't cruel. Just determined.

"I know tactics, Otec. I will help you save your family, though it will cost me everything. But you have to trust me—just long enough for me to get you to Argonholm."

He didn't understand, and he wasn't going to take the time to figure her cryptic words out.

"What's the fastest way to Argonholm?" She pointed at the glacier-topped peaks far above him. "Can we go over the mountain?"

He rose to his feet, ignoring the cramps in his calves. "No one has ever made it all the way over before."

"We have to get to Argonholm, convince them the Raiders will be coming there next. Then send for your father at the coast."

Otec's father. Yes, his father would know what to do—how to save the clan. And just like that, Otec had a purpose. He glanced around, getting his bearings. "This way."

He trotted downhill. Matka kept up without complaint as the morning sun melted the frost and took the sharp bite from the air. Going down was faster than up, but it wore on his legs until they trembled with every step. Matka tried to get him to stop and drink—even take a mouthful of food. But he ignored her, pressing down the mountain until his legs gave out on him. He tried to stand again, but he shook so badly he couldn't.

Matka shoved him down onto his backside. "You're desert sick." She held out the water skin. "Small sips."

"Desert sick?" Otec panted as he took a drink.

She plopped down beside him. "Your body is shutting down because it's overheated and thirsty." She pulled off her boots and dumped out a few rocks. He noticed her socks were bloody. "Trust me, I know a few things about running in the heat," she said.

"But there aren't any deserts in Svassheim," Otec pointed out.

She grabbed his water skin and took a long drink. "How do you know? You've never been there."

"I've seen maps. Talked to sailors at the spring clan feast." He shrugged, this wasn't important. Not now. He pushed himself up and tested his balance. He could stand, but he still felt wobbly.

"We have to go slower," Matka said.

"Why is it you aren't collapsing?"

"I'm used to running. And I've been drinking and eating a bit."

After that, Matka made sure he drank water, and they kept to a walk or an easy jog. Finally, they neared the canyon floor. The Argon and Shyle clans were about a day's journey in either direction. The road was deserted and quiet. Otec could hear nothing over the running river.

"We need to keep out of sight," Matka whispered.

"How did they get so far inland without anyone seeing them?" he asked, his gaze straying in the direction of his village.

Matka shook her head. "I don't know." She slipped along the base of the mountain.

Taking his bow in hand, Otec grudgingly followed her. "The road is faster."

"Yes. But the first thing the army would do is block escape points and post enough men to prevent a counterattack."

"How do you know so much?"

It took her a moment to answer. "At the school I attended, I showed a proclivity toward herbs and healing, so that was my focus. But all of us learned the arts of war."

She froze suddenly and lowered to a crouch, gesturing for him to do the same. He followed her gaze up into the trees to find a white owl with black striations. It was the exact same owl from before. Otec was sure of it, if for no other reason than the way it stared at Matka. "But I buried it. I put a huge rock on the grave."

Matka clenched her fists, fury and hatred rolling from her in waves. Finally, she glared at the bird. Otec had a feeling she had never acknowledged the creature before now. After a moment of what looked like intense listening, she eased back toward him and whispered, "There are Idarans about a quarter league ahead of us."

Forcing himself to look away from the owl, he strained his senses but heard and saw nothing. "How do you know?" he whispered back just as quietly.

She ignored his question. "It will be nightfall soon. Better for us to rest now, eat something, and try to slip past them in the coming dark."

Otec scrubbed his hands over his face, wishing his brothers were here. They'd know what to do. "The two of us could handle a couple of sentinels."

"There are more than that—I'd guess a hundred Idarans."

He ground his teeth. "I'll not rest while the Raiders have my family."

When he made to move around Matka, she grabbed his arm. "Otec, you have to trust me."

He whipped around to face her. "Why? I barely know you."

"I'm trying to help you."

He looked back down the trail, trying to see what she had seen. But then he glanced up at the owl, which stared at him this time.

51

Otec shuddered and followed Matka. They settled down beneath the huge limbs of a pine tree and shared a small meal of travel bread, dried fruit, and meat. She lay down, her eyes closed, but he could tell by her irregular breathing that she wasn't asleep.

He didn't sleep either, unable to stop worrying about his family, imagining various torments while he hid safely beneath a tree.

When it was almost dark, Matka suddenly sat up. With the moon nearly full, he could make out the determination and dread on her face. "Time to go."

As they crossed the ridge of the mountain face, Otec finally saw the men in the trees. Trying to skirt them, he and Matka climbed the mountain again. She was leading the way when she suddenly crouched and motioned for him to do the same. After a moment of listening intently to something he couldn't hear, she silently urged him to go back the way they'd come.

He clenched his jaw but obeyed, and she followed. After a hundred paces, she touched his shoulder. He paused and she came up beside him, leaning in to whisper in his ear. "The Idarans have posted sentinels all the way up to where the cliffs start. We're going to have to backtrack and find another way over."

It took everything in Otec not to scream in frustration. "By then, it will be too late to help anyone. And the Raiders will have infiltrated all of the clan lands."

Matka dropped her head, her expression hidden by shadows. "You won't slip past them, especially not under a full moon. They are not just Idaran army—they're Immortals."

"What?" The most lethal soldiers in the entire world had attacked his village. "How could you possibly know this?"

She dropped her head. "I heard them."

"I was right next to you," Otec replied slowly, "and I saw and heard nothing." She had been acting so strangely since the attack. He realized he knew Matka the artist, and Matka the woman, but he did not know Matka the warrior. And he wasn't sure he could trust her.

He rose from a crouch and started off. She reached for him, but he shook her off. "You don't have to come with me. But I'm going. If I have to fight my way through."

"Otec," she whisper-shouted. "You're no good to anyone if you're dead!"

"I would rather die trying to save my family than live on having done nothing." He took off at a run, using his long legs to outdistance her. When he reached the place she had stopped earlier, he paused, listening. He saw no sentinels, but he slipped slowly through the shadows, making not a sound. His already-exhausted muscles trembled from fatigue, and sweat poured down his face.

He came to a place where the trees thinned so that the mountainside was bare. If there were sentinels, this is where they would be. He hesitated, sensing someone was there.

From behind him, Matka lightly touched his arm. When he looked back, she shook her head, a stray bit of moonlight catching the plea in her eyes.

Otec motioned for her to stay behind while he went ahead, then slipped to his belly and crawled forward. No sooner had he entered the clearing than something seemed to burst beside him. His head whipped around in time to see an arrow glancing off the rocks right next to him.

A shrill whistle cut through the silence. Otec was already up and running. If he could just get past the sentinels, he might be able to stay ahead of the Raiders long enough to warn the other clans.

But as he approached the tree line, three Raiders charged from the trees, their heads shaved to reveal a dizzying pattern of tattoos across their scalps. Otec skidded to a stop, lifting his bow.

Another arrow whizzed past him, making him belatedly dodge to the side. There were archers in the trees! He rolled behind a log and forced himself to think.

When the sentinels charged him, the archers wouldn't be able to shoot for fear of hitting one of their own. Otec had to defeat the three sentinels and make a run for it. Hearing their measured steps approach, he took three arrows in his hand and forced himself to wait. As soon as they were close enough, he rose up and let an arrow fly.

Then another. Then another. Otec was running again. But more Immortals were charging him. He had time to fire one last arrow before they were on him. He whipped out his bow, using it like a staff.

One soldier dropped back, hacking a curved sword down on Otec's bow. Two more swung at him, one from each side. He jumped back, feeling more than seeing the damage to his bow. They tried to encircle him.

Knowing he was dead if they managed it, he backed up, using the much longer reach of his bow to whack at one of the others. The Raider twisted to the side, trapping Otec's bow in his armpit and hacking it in two.

Otec dropped the useless bit of wood, realizing he was finished. But he would die fighting. He charged the Immortal in front of him. The man whipped around Otec, took hold of his neck, and shoved him face down into the dirt. When Otec opened his eyes, the Immortal held a sword tip to his face. Otec didn't know whether he was more shocked that he was about to die or that the Immortal who'd bested him was a woman.

As she pulled back to stab him, terror coursed through his body. He did not want to die. Not like this. But then a voice cut through the stillness and the Immortal paused. Though none of the sentinels moved their swords from him, all of them turned to face the source of the voice.

Otec's eyes widened in horror at the sight of Matka. "Run!" he commanded her, wanting to shake her for coming after him only to get herself killed by an archer.

Then she spoke again, but he recognized none of the words. And he realized she was not speaking Clannish. But he was certain it wasn't Svass either.

The woman holding the sword to Otec's throat responded in the same language. His gaze darted back to Matka. She was speaking Idaran.

Otec stared at her, horror clawing through his chest. "Matka?"

She turned to face him, surrounded by people with dusky skin and shaved scalps. And he knew. She wasn't tan—she was dark skinned. And her hair was short because she'd shaved it before.

"You're an Idaran."

8

atka didn't deny it. And if she was an Idaran, so were Jore and all the rest of the so-called highmen. The Raiders hadn't invaded the Shyle, they'd infiltrated it. And the Shyle had felt safe because half of the visitors' numbers were women.

Otec's rage started on the back of his neck and prickled down his arms. "You came to my people claiming to be friends and made us trust you. And then you attacked us." His voice trembled with barely controlled fury. "But why befriend me—help me—only to do this?" He met Matka's gaze. "What kind of heartless witch are you?"

She winced and barked something at the sentinels, who barked back at her. Whatever she had said worked. While one sentinel kept a sword to Otec's throat, the others bound his hands behind his back, checked him for weapons, and removed his bedroll, which they tossed to the side like it was filled with refuse.

All the while he couldn't help but wonder if these were the same weapons used to kill his friends and family. The same ropes they'd used to bind his family's hands as they'd made them slaves.

They hauled Otec up and shoved him in front of them. With his hands bound, it was hard to keep his balance, and he stumbled down the mountain in the dark. They passed more sentinels and archers in the trees, which must have been how they'd spotted him in the first place. What he wouldn't pay to see them all suffer for what they had done.

A shadowy figure came running at them, calling out to Matka. Otec didn't realize it was Jore until she started shouting at him in Svass. One of the sentinels issued a command. When Matka replied, her voice was softer, but the outrage still came through.

"My family," Otec said pleadingly as Jore approached. "What of my family?"

The man wouldn't look at him. "Those who fought were killed. But your family was all alive when I left."

"Left?" Otec blurted.

One of the guards cuffed him. "Silence!"

Jore stepped closer and dropped his voice so the other sentinels couldn't hear. "Their guards have no reason to harm your family so long as they remain compliant."

Otec spit at Jore, who wiped his face without showing any reaction. "I told you to remember," Jore said without looking back.

Matka stormed up to her brother, shoving him and cursing him in Svass. Jore kept his balance and spoke to her in a low tone.

Ignoring them, the guards dragged Otec into a campsite tucked deep into a grove. There were no tents. No fires. Hardly any sounds. Just dozens and dozens of Raiders sleeping in blankets as if they hadn't just murdered women and children and burned their homes to the ground.

The sentinels directed Otec to stand before a figure curled up in blankets. They said something in Idaran, and a man shifted and pulled the blankets off his head.

It was Tyleze, the man who'd commanded Jore to stand down after he'd insulted Holla. "What's this?" he asked.

"Tyleze," Matka blurted as she stumbled up behind Otec. "You promised me!"

Tyleze yawned and looked up at them. "You should be grateful, Matka. We could have used your help in the midst of battle—the clanwomen might have been unprepared, but they fought like hyenas. We very nearly lost."

"I should have been there," Otec said to Matka under his breath, his voice the heat of embers right before they burst into flame. "Because of you I wasn't."

She turned her face away from him.

"Why isn't he dead?" Tyleze said tiredly.

The sentinels spoke Idaran in hushed voices, and Tyleze's brow climbed higher with every word. Finally he turned his gaze to Matka. He asked a question, which she answered, her head held high and not a trace of fear on her face. Otec only understood one word: "priestess."

Tyleze grunted and gestured to Otec, who unconsciously stiffened. Matka answered the man, her voice more insistent this time, but he only waved his hand. The guards took hold of Otec's shoulders, pulling him away.

Matka shot him a desperate look, a tear spilling down her cheek. She brushed the moisture quickly away, so quickly he almost wondered if it had been there at all. Otec didn't understand why she would betray him and then try to save him. He didn't know why she'd dragged him into all of this in the first place. He only knew that whatever she had tried to do to save him had failed. He was going to die. But by the Balance, he would take some of them with him.

"I mark you for the dead, Matka." It was an old curse; yesterday he would have called it a superstition. Today, he hoped it was real. For it was the only way he had left that could hurt her. "I mark you all for the dead."

"I was marked a long time ago," she said in a low, shaking voice.

The guards wrenched Otec around, each holding one of his arms. He saw where they were heading—a small clearing with a dead, lightning-struck tree in the center. They shoved him to his knees. One held his hair and pinned his head down. The other raised his sword.

The horror inside Otec sharpened, until he felt all his emotions bleed out of him, leaving a hollowed-out husk. He looked into the dark night, wanting the last thing he ever saw to be the forests of his homeland.

But what he saw was the owl, staring past him to where Matka was standing. "Very well," Matka said. "You have my word."

It raised its wings and dove forward. Otec craned his neck in time to see Matka toss a bag at the creature. It caught the bag in its talons. More owls flew from the trees, and Matka threw a bag at each of them before they disappeared.

Then the man holding the sword over Otec grunted, the breath hissing out of him. The other guard gave a shout and reached behind him for his own swords. Matka charged, her blades thrusting into the guard's belly. He dropped to the ground, his feet kicking.

"Hold out your hands." Matka's voice was strangely calm.

Questions tumbled in Otec's mind, but right now there wasn't time for any of them. He held his hands out and she shoved her sword between them and jerked it up. The blade nicked the sides of his palms as it snapped through the ropes. Otec didn't feel any pain, only warm, sticky blood seeping between his hands.

"What are you doing?" he asked, dumbfounded.

Matka reached down and hauled him up. "Move." She shoved a knife into his hands.

"We'll never get away. We're outnumbered five hundred to two."

She gave a slight shake of her head. "No. But their help will cost me. Goddess, grant that I might bear that cost."

Before Otec could ask what she meant, fire exploded through the trees in flames of green, blue, and purple.

"Come on!" she cried as she darted forward without waiting to see if he would follow. As if she wasn't afraid he would stab her in the back with the knife she'd given him.

But even as the thought flitted through his head, he knew she was right not to fear him—he couldn't harm her. And not just because she was a woman.

More fire erupted as they skirted the camp. Raiders yelled and ran, trying to escape the flames that seemed to crop up everywhere. Everywhere except where Otec and Matka ran.

Finally, they left the last of the fires behind and ran full tilt down the road in the smoky gray light.

"What was that?" he gasped.

"Luminash. Something only priestesses have access to."

"How is it everywhere?"

"The owls."

Otec didn't know how to respond, and by then he was breathing too hard to try.

They slowed when he could taste blood in his mouth, but Matka did not pause to rest, simply trotted on and on as if she'd never stop. It took everything Otec had to keep up.

She passed him her water skin. "Small sips."

She was obviously Idaran, so why would she help him? And since she was helping him, why hadn't she warned him about the attack sooner? "Matka—"

"As soon as the Idarans off the coast realized the Shyle had fallen, they would have struck."

"Attacking the clans from two fronts," Otec choked out.

Matka nodded, then took the water skin and drank deep. "Come on, we have to go faster."

He did as she asked, watching her study the road behind them. "If you're Idaran, why are you helping me?"

"Are you sure I am one of them?" she said, her words clipped.

Her anger fueled his own. He grabbed her arm and wrenched her around, breaking open the shallow cuts on his palms. She didn't fight him as he tipped her head toward the predawn light and lifted the strands of her short hair and saw the tattoos on her scalp. "I'm sure."

Otec shoved her away. "My clanmen are dead." It hurt him to say it, down to the bones. "You could have prevented it if you had told me!"

"You think you could have stopped five hundred Immortals?" She turned away and started up again. Otec had no choice but to keep up. It infuriated him that while he was out of breath and stumbling, she seemed completely unaffected.

"I was trying to get them to call off the invasion—to realize Idara is not superior. That's why Jore was angry that day by the forest. I'd pushed too hard too many times. He was afraid they would kill me for it. That night, Tyleze told me to go with you into the mountains. He said the ships were turning back because of storms at sea."

Matka wiped under her eyes again. "I was a fool for believing them, but I wanted to so badly." She winced when she caught Otec glaring at her. "I won't apologize for taking you away. They would have killed you, and then there would be no one to warn the rest of the clan lands."

After all the time he'd spent with her, he still didn't know her. "Why would you, an Idaran, risk your life to help me?"

An expression of exquisite pain overtook her face. "My mother was a highwoman slave. Only when I was taken by the priestesses did my father even bother to learn my name. So you tell me, Otec, whether I am an Idaran or a highwoman."

He was torn between wanting to believe her and wanting to hate her, yet the vulnerability on her face was unmistakable. "And Jore? Is he a highman too?"

Matka shook her head. "No. He believes the world would be a better place if Idara ruled it."

Otec ground his teeth. "If ever I see him again—"

"You don't know everything about him." Her head fell. "We had a sister like Holla once. She disappeared one night and we never saw her again."

"By the Balance." Perhaps that explained Jore's hatred of Holla. Whenever he'd looked at her, he must have been reminded of the sister who'd been murdered.

"My other sister is an acolyte in the Temple of Fire," Matka went on. "She's too young to remember being a servant in my father's house. Sleeping in the blistering attic while my father shared the lower levels with his wife and children, who hated and reviled us. Suka is determined to be the next high priestess. And she'll probably get it."

"Are you really half highman?" Otec asked.

"It's the reason all of us were chosen for this assignment. We could speak and pass for highmen among the clan lands." For a time, there was only the sound of the breathing and their footfalls. "I know you don't trust me, Otec. I don't blame you. But I am trying to help you."

He didn't say anything—he didn't have the words.

And then something whooshed over their heads. It was the owl. Matka tensed, hesitating before ripping her satchel over her shoulder and thrusting it into Otec's hands. "There's luminash inside—you might need it." Then she yanked her swords out and whipped around. "Keep going! I'll catch up."

He turned to see Jore charging them. "Matka!" Jore growled, his swords held loosely in his hands. His mouth was compressed in a tight line, his expression thunderous with anger as he scolded her in Idaran.

Matka answered in Clannish. "The king thinks he's bringing order to chaos. Knowledge to ignorance—but the clan lands don't need either! They're good and kind and—"

"Traitor," Jore ground out as he stopped a few paces from them.

She straightened her shoulders. "I am a priestess of the Temple of Fire. I do not serve Idara. I serve the Goddess of Fire. And this goes against her laws of life and growth."

"Let the flames consume the dross so that only the pure remain," Jore said as if by rote.

Matka briefly closed her eyes. "I've made my choice, Jore. I will serve the Light. Now you must make yours."

"Matka," he began in a softer tone, "let me kill him. No one will have to know you helped him. We'll tell them he killed Bez and Harim and then escaped, and you went after him."

"They'll never believe it." Her voice shook, but her swords did not. More softly, she said to Otec, "He won't harm me. Go, before the rest of them come."

"We'll subdue him together," Otec said.

"I'm not going to let you ruin your life for a man whose country won't even exist in a few months," Jore growled. And then he lunged, but Matka met his thrust with a lightning-fast parry.

All Otec had was the knife she had slipped him, and he dared not throw it for fear of hitting her. He searched for a stick long enough to whack Jore on the back of the head.

Jore and Matka danced around each other, their blades twisting sinuously around their bodies, which were backlit by the coming dawn. Jore feinted to the right, reversed, and came at her from the side. She blocked him. Barely.

Jore was faster, stronger, better. Matka was going to lose. Abandoning his search, Otec gripped the knife and tried to sneak up behind Jore. The man turned suddenly, his sword arching for Otec's side. Matka jumped between them. Jore's eyes widened and he tried to pull back, but it was too late to stop his momentum.

The owl dove between them, taking the full thrust in its middle. Pinned to Matka's chest by Jore's sword, it looked up at Matka as it died.

She met its gaze, her expression shocked and wary. Jore stepped back, shaking the dead bird from his blade. Otec tried to tackle him, but Jore sidestepped, his swords arcing down.

Matka darted between them and locked blades with Jore. She managed to throw him off. Barely. "Stay out of the way," she growled at Otec, sweat pouring down her temples as she charged.

He backed away, feeling horrified and useless—his "help" had almost gotten Matka killed. His head came up at a shout from the direction of the enemy camp. It was close enough he knew he would see Raiders any moment.

"Go," Matka gasped as she retreated. "The others won't be far behind. I'll hold them off as long as I can."

Otec opened his mouth to reply when he heard another shout, even closer this time. He hesitated, not wanting to leave her. "Go to Argonholm," she ordered between breaths. "Get help."

Otec thought of his family. Enemy or friend, Otec couldn't save Matka. Not if he was going to save his family. He started running.

9

At midday, Otec kicked the horse he'd demanded from a farmer into Argonholm. "Raiders! Raiders!" Otec cried out as he went. All around him, doors were thrown open, and people in the streets stared after him. He saw no warriors—they too must have gone to defend against the Raiders on the coast.

As Otec reached the clan house, Seneth hurried out to meet him, coughing violently in his hand. The only son of the Argon clan chief, Seneth was around the same age of Otec's oldest brother, Dagen.

Seneth's wife, Narium, who was heavy with child, hurried after him, reaching out as if to catch him should he fall. "Your fever's only just broken. Come back inside."

He held out a hand to silence her. "Otec?" he managed through his wheezing. "What is it?"

Otec jumped down from the horse. "Raiders attacked the Shyle two nights ago."

Seneth shook his head. "Raiders couldn't have come this far inland."

A crowd was forming around them. "The visiting highmen were actually Raiders. They plan to hit us from two fronts."

"That's impossible!" Seneth cried.

Otec forced himself to meet the older man's gaze. "Shyle has fallen."

Seneth glanced back at the clan house. "My father—the other men—they're all gone."

Narium stepped forward and spoke low. "Come inside. You're scaring the children."

Otec looked around and realized she was right. The Argons were mostly a scattering of wide-eyed children, steel-eyed women, and older men. Seneth motioned for Otec to follow him as they turned toward the clan house.

"Gather up anyone who can fight," Narium called back to her people. "Meet in the great hall."

They stepped into the clan house's kitchen, which was larger than the Shyle's, even though this was home to fewer people. Otec thought of all the times he'd sat at his family's ancient kitchen table, wishing for silence. Now he'd give anything to be home, with dozens of children running and shrieking around him.

After pushing Otec into a chair, Narium handed him a cup of the Argon's legendary beer, and gave Seneth a cup of something that smelled like honey and licorice.

"Send a couple of pigeons to High Chief Burdin. He'll tell my father and Hargar." Seneth took a careful drink. "I can't believe I had Raiders as guests at my clan house."

Narium set bread and cheese in front of Otec, then took out some fibrous paper, cut it into two strips, and began writing, her characters small and tight.

"Tell them there are five hundred Raiders," Otec said without looking at her. Once his father and brothers were here, everything would be all right. They would defeat the Raiders and free his family.

Seneth gasped. "There weren't that many before!"

"The women were fighting alongside their men," Otec said.

Seneth sat back in his chair, clearly dumbfounded. "That's
—"

"I saw it myself." Otec took a deep pull of his beer, the bit-
terness fanning across his tongue. He heard people filtering into
the great hall.

Lips pressed into a thin line, Seneth made to stand up. Narium put her hands on his shoulders to keep him down. "There's
no point until they're all here."

Seneth cast her a look. "I'm going to have to talk to them
eventually." Trying not to cough had turned his face red.

"Push too hard and you won't be any help to anyone," Narium shot back.

"Don't coddle me," he growled, but she was already halfway to the door that led outside. Seneth turned to Otec. "Tell me
everything that happened."

Otec relayed the important parts. Then he pulled out Matka's satchel, which he'd gone through earlier. The food was long
gone. Left were her drawing tools—charcoal, board, vellum, and
extra paper—worthless bits without the magic of her touch. A
few of her drawings, mostly plants. But there was also the drawing of the Shyle. Otec's village would never be the same, now
that the Raiders had burned and violated it.

The flower Otec had carved for Matka was gone; she must
have kept it with her. He was glad. He had a piece of her, and
now she had a piece of him.

Her satchel also contained some small bags of a sharp-
smelling powder, which Otec explained must be luminash. Seneth rubbed it between his fingers. "It doesn't look like it's going
to explode."

Otec took a pinch between his thumb and finger and tossed
it onto the coals. It flared a hot, bright white that quickly faded.
He and Seneth stared at the fireplace as if they'd never seen it
before.

They tried each of the four pouches. One burned bright and hot, one burned for a long time, one burned in a multitude of beautiful flames, and the fourth burned orange and long, like an ember.

"This could be very useful," Seneth said, rubbing his throat as if it pained him. "We'll have to send scouts to warn us if the Raiders come out of the pass."

Otec gestured toward the village. "I saw nothing but women and children. Who will you send?"

Seneth hesitated. "The boys the militia left behind. They're faster and lighter than the men anyway."

"They're children," Otec choked out.

"It's that or send the women," Seneth growled. He shot Otec a sheepish look. "I've been sick abed for over a week—it's why I'm here being hounded by my pregnant wife instead of at the front lines with the others." As if to punctuate his words, Seneth started into a coughing fit.

Otec dropped his head, the shame of being purposely left behind burning through him.

Narium reappeared at the doorway. "It's done."

Imagining the fate of his mother and sisters, Otec told Seneth, "You should evacuate the women to Tyron. They'll be safer there."

Seneth stared at his hands before looking up. "They won't be happy about it, but I'll see it's done." He looked at Narium for confirmation. After a brief hesitation, she nodded.

Otec watched them, a sudden pang for Matka's safety shooting through him. Was she dead? Were all the women he cared about dead?

Seneth lumbered to his feet. Legs shaking from exhaustion, Otec followed him into the massive great hall. It was packed with adults, mostly women and a scattering of elder men. All of them stared at him, but he didn't get the familiar sick lump in his stomach. Being intimidated by crowds suddenly seemed a small thing after all he had been through.

Wasting no time, Seneth announced, "The women and children will flee to Tyron."

"Isn't that closer to the armada bearing down on our shores?" asked an older woman.

Seneth eyed her. "There's nothing but a few leagues between a company of five hundred Raiders and our village. Any boy over the age of thirteen will be staying, as will any man strong enough to use a bow or axe. The rest of you have two hours to pack what you need."

An immediate outcry rose up. "No!"

"My boys aren't old enough to go to war!"

"They'll be cut down like wheat before a sickle!"

Seneth held out his hands. "Every single one of them can use a bow and arrow. And they're all we have."

A middle-aged woman stepped forward. "I'll fight in my son's place."

Seneth squeezed his fists tight, the only sign he was frustrated. "And who will raise your other children if your husband dies, Getta? You're needed elsewhere. The boys are faster and stronger."

She opened her mouth to argue.

"A clanwoman does not ask for things she shouldn't," Seneth roared. "You will be leaving in two hours, regardless of how long you stand here arguing with me!"

The younger women were already filing out—they probably didn't have sons old enough to stay. Some of the older women followed them.

Seneth motioned for a couple of women to come forward. "Getta, Allis, I'm going to need your boys to ride for the canyon on the fastest horses we have left. If they see the Raiders coming, they're to light a signal fire and come back at once."

"No," Getta said in a trembling voice. Allis dropped her head as if it weighed too much to hold up.

"Get them both ready," Seneth commanded. "I want them gone within the hour. But send them here first."

Getta clamped her jaw shut.

Allis cast Narium a helpless look. "Please—"

Narium looked into the woman's eyes. "They're the best chance we have, and right now the clan needs them."

The fight seemed to leak out of both women.

Otec marveled at Seneth's resolve. The way he expected his people to follow him—to trust him—to the point where he demanded it. Otec didn't think he could ever do that.

Seneth nodded to Narium. "Help the boys get ready."

Without hesitation she marched out of the room, Allis right behind her. Getta paused before turning to leave, but not before she shot one last glare at Seneth.

As soon as they were gone, Seneth broke into a coughing fit. He stumbled back into the kitchen, where he tried to pour himself another cup of tea with shaky hands. Otec took the pot from him and poured. Seneth took a swallow, wincing when the hot liquid went down. He sank into the chair, out of breath.

"How do you know the women will obey you? You can't really enforce it," Otec said.

Seneth closed his eyes. "I won't have to. The boys are too proud to stay behind now that they're being treated like men."

"Are you in any state to lead?" Otec asked.

Seneth opened his eyes. "Are you?"

"I was never meant to lead. I'm a throw-away son."

Seneth poured more beer into Otec's cup. "Not anymore."

10

Three boys stepped into the clan house. "The twins are Ake and Arvid, Allis's boys," Seneth said. "Getta's boy is Ivar." They stood straight and tall, but one of the twins was obviously terrified. The other had sweat on his brow. Ivar simply seemed excited.

Seneth looked them over. "There are Raiders in the pass. And there's nothing between them and us but a few leagues.

"Mother said we're to watch and light a signal fire if we see any of them," Ivar said with enthusiasm.

"There's a bit more to it than that," Seneth explained. "Even if our clanmen push through a forced march from the coast, it'll take at least four days for them to get here. The Raiders will attack before then. They'd be stupid not to."

One of the twins—Otec couldn't remember which—shifted his weight from one foot to the other, then asked, "What do you want us to do?"

Seneth started coughing again, so it was half a minute before he could answer. "I want you to light the forest on fire. Gather up clusters of dried brush and make a long line. Just be sure the wind is driving the fire up the pass instead of down on us before you start it."

"And if the wind changes direction?" Otec said.

"Then the plan fails." Seneth pointed to the pouch of open luminash on the table. "You're going to use this to do it."

Otec felt the blood drain from his face. Using fire as a weapon was like trying to catch a wild badger—at some point it would turn around and bite. "Seneth—"

"Do you see another way, Otec? Because if you do, I'll gladly take it. As it is, this is as likely to fail as not."

Otec chewed on his lower lip, trying to come up with something else, but what else was there? They had to delay the Raiders while they waited for the clanmen to come, or everything was lost.

"I'm going with them," he said, surprising himself. He couldn't let these children face this alone, and he was done being left behind.

Seneth shot him a look. "Just standing makes you shake."

"Then give me a horse," Otec said, his voice quiet but determined.

Seneth started to grin and then seemed to think better of it. "I'd be no good to you—not with this sickness."

Otec nodded. "Run things here. We'll be back."

Narium appeared at the door. "We're ready."

"Bring out another horse," Seneth said. "Otec is going."

Narium's mouth tightened, but she whirled around and called for another horse by name, then ordered women to gather more food and do it now.

Feeling weak, Otec forced himself to stand. He took the boys outside, where a fourth horse was being brought out.

Seneth stood at the doorway. "Otec, I'm sending a pigeon with you. If . . ." His gaze darted to the mothers, who were wringing their hands and whimpering. He lowered his voice. "I'll set up more watchers, but you have to send the birds back or we won't have enough warning."

Otec understood. If they were captured or killed, Argon-holm wouldn't know until it was too late to flee. "I'll keep them nearby."

Narium brought him the horse. "Your body is going to fail you soon. Let the boys work tonight while you sleep, or you'll be worse than useless." She handed him a couple of herb bags. "The one that smells bad is for nights. The one that tastes bad is for the mornings. A palmful of each."

He stuffed them in his saddlebags. "Thank you, Narium." He swung up into the saddle and rode away as the people of Argonholm frantically packed what they could onto wagons and the backs of horses.

Ivar immediately took the lead, and Otec let him. The boy would learn soon enough that being a man mostly meant extra work and more responsibility. Otec and the boys paced the horses, rotating between walking, trotting, and galloping.

Ake and Arvid were quiet and watchful. "Do you know the canyon well?" Otec asked them. The twins nodded in harmony. "There's a place where the forest is thick and the pass narrow," Otec went on. "We'll make for there. Understand?"

"Yes," the twins said in unison.

Ivar dropped back to ride with Otec. "They're a bit creepy," he muttered under his breath. "But eventually you sort of get used to them."

"You must listen to me, Ivar. I've faced these Raiders, and they are fast and merciless. If I say run, you have to promise me that you will." Otec met the boy's gaze and refused to look away until he agreed. Then Otec glanced back at the twins. "You two as well." Both nodded.

At nightfall, after hours in the saddle, they reached the pass between Argon and Shyle. It was heavily wooded here, with the forest constantly overtaking the wagon-rutted road. Otec sent one of the boys farther up the pass to keep watch; the others he set about gathering anything flammable and laying it on the ground in a long line. Then he went to sleep.

At daybreak, Ake woke Otec to say, "Arvid saw the Raiders. They'll be here by midmorning."

Otec groaned. His legs felt like they were full of sharp-edged gravel. He rubbed them down while one of the twins handed him the tea Narium had packed for him, plus a slice of bread slathered with butter and blackberry jam. By the time he'd eaten he could move, though it still hurt and he walked with a limp. He glanced at the long line of sticks and brush the boys had managed to make during the night.

He took out the four bags of luminash, preparing to tell the boys how to use it, when Arvid came running through the heavy trees. "There are scouts at the front—a dozen of them. They'll be here any moment!"

Otec tried to peer through the thick forest. It was innocent and beautiful . . . and waiting to be burned. "Light the torches!" When Ivar didn't move, Otec shoved him toward the horses, which were tethered in a meadow behind them. "Go!"

Running, Otec began spreading the powder onto the line of sticks and brush. The luminash clung to his sweat and burned the shallow cuts on his palms as it billowed out like fine dust. With one bag emptied, he glanced back at the boys, who still struggled to light a torch.

He heard a shout and glanced past the boys to see a dozen Raiders bearing down on them. Abandoning the line of debris, Otec sprinted toward the boys. "Back to the horses. Let the pigeon go." The twins abandoned their kindling and rushed toward the horses.

Ivar still hunched over his kindling. "I have a coal." He blew on it, determination written on his round face.

Otec stepped protectively in front of him, drawing his bow. He let loose an arrow, but it imbedded in a tree instead of a

Raider. He wouldn't have a clear shot until the enemy was nearly upon them. "Ivar, go now!"

The boy blew gently, his hands shaking. Smoke surrounded his head as hungry flames rose and began to lick up the kindling. Otec turned to face the Raiders, letting loose three arrows as they sloshed through the river, but only managed to hit one man. Two dozen steps and the Raiders would be on them. Otec couldn't stop eleven of them.

Ivar had touched the torch to the fragile frames. "Throw it!" Otec shouted.

Ivar hurtled the torch into the luminash-dusted debris. It flared bright, a blast of heat that sent Otec reeling.

He glanced through smoke and flames to see the Raiders hurtled backward. The fire flashed along the kindling, stopping where he had stopped spreading luminash when he'd run back to protect the boys. Otec clenched his teeth. "Come on, burn!" But there was no wind, and the flames consumed the trees but didn't spread beyond them.

The Raiders split into two groups. Half moved around the fire to come at the clanmen from below. The other half drew back their bows.

Otec hauled another bag out of his pocket and raced to the line of fire. Arrows began raining down. He ran faster, barely limping. But it wasn't going to be enough. They were going to stop him. They were going to put out the flames.

And then a white blur shot past him, snatching the bag of powder out of his hands. The owl's sharp beak tore a small hole in the bag, and powder flowed out in a thin stream like sand from an hourglass. The fire flashed after the luminash, ate up the powder as it fell from the sky, and collided with a tree still covered in dry autumn leaves. The tree burst into flames, thick smoke churning up and turning the sun blood red.

One of the Raiders skidded to a halt, "Luminash is sacred!" Fury cast harsh lines across his face. He brought up his bow, aiming for the owl.

Otec loaded an arrow. "Ivar! Help me!" The boy loosed an arrow, which sliced into a Raider, sending him to his knees.

Otec released his arrow, feeling the twang of the bow as it vibrated in his hand. The Raider who had taken aim at the owl staggered back, an arrow in his chest. Otec felt no sorrow, no regret. Only a bone-deep satisfaction. He drew back and released another arrow. And another.

The owl returned, talons open, and Otec tossed her another bag. She caught it and pivoted in midair, her beak tearing a hole as she whirled about. Then the twins were beside Otec on their horse, releasing arrow after arrow.

With the owl's help, the fire spread farther up the pass, devouring the distance to the Raiders, who turned and ran as the smoke stalked them, the fire feeding a growing wind that howled after them.

When the owl had spread all the luminash, she landed on a lower limb of a tree, far away from the flames, and looked at Otec as if waiting.

Without breaking eye contact with her, he said to the boys, "Stay here, and whatever you do, don't look at the owl." Matka had refused to look—she'd been terrified of it.

"I killed men?" Ivar said.

Otec turned back to find the boy shaking, his previous confidence gone.

"Ake, Arvid, get him back to Argonholm. Let them know the pigeon was wrong. The fire will hold them."

"How do you—" Ake began.

"Go now!" Otec ordered.

Once they had turned their mounts and galloped away, he approached the owl and stopped before it, his horse dancing restlessly beneath him. The bird watched him with far too much intelligence. As soon as Otec thought this, the owl shivered, its body shimmering. The feathers shrank and disappeared, leaving behind slate-purple skin and a human-like face with black lips. She wore a short, feathered dress, and her hair was snow white with black tips. Her long ears pointed away from her head. But her eyes were still yellow, and the wings on her back still resembled those of an owl.

"You're a fairy," Otec said in disbelief. This was the creature that had terrorized Matka, the creature that had somehow warned her the night she was captured.

"You are the only man I have ever revealed myself to. You should feel privileged." The fairy's voice was deep and her words clipped.

"You're the darkness that follows Matka."

The fairy cocked her head to the side in a movement so bird-like it made Otec shudder. "No. I am simply the one who brings about the end," she declared.

"The end?"

She shook out her feathers. "An end is required to bring about a new beginning. But endings are always messy, and they require a breaking. If mankind survives, everything will be different."

If Otec was wary before, he was terrified now. "Why are you helping me?"

She seemed to look into his soul then, examining its flaws, vices, and strengths beneath her clawed fingertips. It took everything he had to look away, and when he did, he felt violated and wronged, like he needed to scrub his body with fire to get rid of the feeling.

"I have saved your life, and the lives of your friends. In return, you will save Matka," the fairy announced.

"Of course I'll save her!"

The fairy's wings stretched out behind her. "Good, then the bargain is struck." She launched herself from the branch.

"Bargain?" Otec called after her. "What bargain?"

Hovering, she looked back at him as if he was daft. "In the game of fire, every person is a player, and the world the field."

"Game of fire?" he said in bewilderment.

The fairy smiled, cruel and terrible. "All the pieces are in place now. Over the next twenty years, the game will play out exactly how I want it, if you manage to keep your end of the bargain. If you fail, the curse you placed upon Matka will devour you."

"I didn't mean it!" Otec blurted. "I thought she had betrayed me! You must remove the curse."

The fairy narrowed her eyes at him. "You have brought upon her the attention of the dead, which is not within my power to remove. I will see that Matka accomplishes her move. Then the dead will take her."

"No," Otec begged. "Please!"

Feathers emerged from the fairy's body, growing as feet were replaced with talons. A mouth with a beak. Hair with feathers. She flapped her wings, then caught an updraft from the raging fire and soared out of sight past the line of smoke.

11

Otec lay beside a smoldering campfire, staring up at stars that were too weak to give off any useful light. Sharing a room with three brothers used to feel suffocating. But now that he was alone, he could barely close his eyes lest the emptiness steal in with the dark and smother him with loss and loneliness.

Sleep had become a specter in the night—a quarry to be endlessly chased but never caught. So Otec stared at the useless stars until he heard distant hoof beats. A sharp whinny broke out from one of his horses. Otec pushed himself up as Ake stepped into the dim firelight and said, "Clanmen are approaching."

The boy, who'd been on watch, should have brought the warning long before Otec could hear their horses. "Did you fall asleep?"

Ake dropped his head. "I'm sorry, Otec."

Moving stiffly, Otec pulled back his furs and tugged his boots onto his swollen and blistered feet. He pushed himself to a stand, his muscles sore down to the bone. He looked up at the uncaring stars and realized he must be like them. "Had they been Raiders, we'd all be dead."

He moved past the boy without another word, squinting at the canyon. It was too dark to see the smoke, but Otec could smell it, dark and heavy. Knowing he would need more light, he tossed logs on the fire as the clanmen drew closer. A minute later they came into camp, dark figures on blowing horses. The men dismounted and stepped into the growing light.

First, Otec saw Seneth, who nodded a greeting and then moved to the fire. Otec's father, Hargar, stepped forward. Otec looked at the other men, searching for his three brothers.

"Rest the animals and eat something," Hargar said to his men. "We'll move out in an hour." His gaze fell on his son. Motioning for Otec to follow, he stepped away from the others and sat heavily on a rotting tree trunk.

Otec sat beside him and searched the faces of the men still moving into the encampment.

"Your brothers are dead." Hargar said.

Otec's head whipped up. "Which ones?"

"Lok and Frey both died on the battlefield. Dagen died of his wounds five days later." Tears streamed down Hargar's face and disappeared in his gray beard.

Otec desperately shook his head. "No. They're too strong and cunning and—"

"They're dead, boy. I buried them together in a single grave, so their bones wouldn't be alone."

Otec stared into the depthless sky, feeling like he was falling. Desperate for something to occupy his hands, he picked up his knife and a bit of wood he'd been working on, carving a little field mouse. But the eyes were wrong—eerie and far too large for the face.

Flinching as if in pain, Hargar removed his battle axe, specially made of solid steel, and leaned it on the tree trunk beside them. "What happened to my clan?"

Otec wiped his eyes so he could see his carving. "I was in the mountains with the highwoman Matka. Do you remember her?" When his father nodded, Otec went on, "We saw the fires and went for help."

He couldn't look at his father as he said this, for the shame that ate away at his insides. "It turns out she wasn't a highwoman at all, but an Idaran. Still, she risked her life to free me."

Hargar rested a heavy hand on Otec's back. "Seneth told me what you did at the canyon. I've brought nearly seventy boys from all over the clan lands. I'm going to use them as archers. And I want you to lead them."

Otec looked at Ake and Ivar and Arvid. He'd lead them, yes, but his only goal was to keep them alive. Heading into battle with nearly a hundred boys . . . "Father, I don't know how."

"Don't be so selfish," Hargar growled.

"Selfish?"

"Yes, selfish!" Hargar gestured to the men who had gathered around the fire. Some were cooking. Others lay on the ground, resting. "Being a leader isn't about you—it's about them."

Otec shook his head in frustration. "But what if I get them killed?"

His father passed a hand over his face, and Otec noticed how haggard he was. His eyes were bloodshot, and a bandage covered most of his left arm. "I say again—it isn't about you. It's about what's best for everyone."

Otec stared at his hands. "I—I don't think I'm the best man to lead them. Surely there's someone with more experience."

"You'll be the next clan chief now. You'll have to learn fast."

Suddenly dizzy, Otec leaned forward. "I'm not supposed to lead."

His father batted the little wooden mouse out of Otec's hands. It skittered across some rocks, one of the delicate ears broken off. Otec's palm stung where the whittling knife had cut into him. "It's time to put away childish things," Hargar said. He went to one of the horses and removed an axe, then returned and held it out to Otec. "Let's go and get our family."

Otec stretched out his hand and took the axe, which felt foreign and impossibly heavy. His father marched toward the fire and settled down on the furs Otec had vacated. Otec opened his palm to look at the smear his cut had left on the haft. How fitting that the first blood the weapon had worn was his own. He stood to follow, but not before he retrieved the little mouse and placed it deep in his pocket. He sat beside his father and glanced at the clanmen. They had just made a five-day trip in less than three, and their faces were hard with determination and exhaustion.

Hargar motioned for Otec to eat, so he forced down the lumpy gruel, which tasted like wet ashes. His father slurped his own gruel, then said, "This attack was well planned. The Raiders struck my village and the coast on the same day."

"Will we hold?" Seneth asked.

Undon, the eldest son of the Tyron clan chief, leaned forward. "They hit Cardenholm first, but the city held fast—which is vital, as that would have given them control over most of the river ways."

Hargar grunted. "They struck Corholm next. They outnumbered us two to one, and we couldn't hold it."

"How many men have you brought?" Otec asked.

Hargar drank a cup of beer, his throat working. He set the cup down with a smack and wiped his face. "High Chief Burdin would only allow two hundred and fifty of us—most of the Shyle as well as a few Tyrons commanded by Undon, and Argons commanded by Seneth. Any more, and Reisenholm would never stand against them."

Otec spread his hand wide. "Why didn't they allow more of the Shyle clanmen? Surely they wouldn't abandon us now."

Hargar grunted. "The rest are on the other side of the clan lands, in Delia. They couldn't have gotten here in time."

Otec rested his pounding head on his palms. "So the Raiders outnumber us two to one." By the Balance, how was he going to keep all these boys alive to go back home to their mothers?

His father slapped his back, making his head pound even harder. "We know the land, and that gives us the advantage." He turned to Seneth. "Will the boys be ready to fight?"

Seneth stared at his bowl. "They'll have to be."

"Good. Battles makes men out of boys. And men are what we need now." Hargar glanced at Otec as he said this, then just as quickly looked away. With sudden vigor, Otec's father pushed to his feet.

Otec stared at the remnants of lumpy gruel in his bowl, wishing he hadn't forced himself to finish.

"Mount up," he said. "Let's move."

"That wasn't an hour," someone grumbled.

"After we've moved into place," his father growled, "you can rest until it's time to kill Raiders."

That bought a cheer. Otec stepped up to his borrowed horse, saddled him quickly, and mounted up. Seneth rode next to him. "Dagen—" he started after a minute.

"Don't," Otec said. He couldn't deal with his grief and the impending battle at the same time.

They climbed into the pass, the horses with their superior night vision picking their way along the blackened path. Patches of embers still burned where trees had been, glowing white-yellow when the breeze picked up. The horse's hoofs kicked up ash, which grew into a cloud that coated Otec's skin and left him with the taste of burning.

When they reached the place just beyond the canyon summit, Seneth called out to the men around them, "The Raiders think to strike us just before dawn. They believe us trapped, that outnumbering us two to one ensures their victory, but they forget that we know our lands. We could hold their five hundred in those mountains with a mere hundred men. But lucky for us, we have over two hundred."

The clanmen all hit the flat of their axes against their shields.

Hargar stepped forward and spoke without any trace of the devastation Otec had witnessed earlier. "We will secrete ourselves in the forests at the narrowest part of the pass while the boys ambush them from above. Then we will hold our ground until every last one of them is dead."

Over two hundred men cheered—angry, bloodthirsty cheers. Otec stayed silent, the weight of his father's expectations oppressively heavy.

12

The clanmen chose a narrow place in the mountain pass where the fire had been blocked from the forest by the river on one side and a cliff on the other. Sometime in the night, the weather had changed, shifting from the spice of autumn to the chill of winter as dark clouds billowed across the turbulent sky.

Concealed behind a bare outcropping of rock, Otec felt the outline of the broken little mouse in his pocket as he lay waiting, shivering, with the boys of the Tyron and Argon clans in the hours before dawn. All were silent and still, anticipating the signal from Otec's father, who hid with the men behind a rise in the road. They would prevent the Raiders from entering Argon, while the boys fired from above.

Otec just hoped he didn't get any of the boys killed. A clanman learned the art of the bow from the time he could walk, but these boys had never fought in a real battle before, and he'd never been a leader.

He heard a scuffle behind him and turned to reprimand the boys, since the Raiders would come into view any second. The twins had pinned another boy down. It was Ivar, his eyes wide, like those of a spooked cart horse that is determined to run, no matter who or what it plows over. "I can't do this again," he cried loudly. "I can't kill another man, even a Raider!"

One of the twins clapped a hand over Ivar's mouth. "You fool! You'll get us all killed."

Every man had to face his fear. For the twins, the fear had come first. For Ivar, it was coming now. Seeing the panic in the child's face, something within Otec hardened. "I have killed Raiders," he said. "They die just as easily as a deer or a lamb, and they are more a beast than both." The boys all looked at him, and he so desperately wanted to say something to rally them— something like Seneth and his father had said earlier. For some reason, Otec thought of Matka on that cliff, terrified and alone.

"Though you are still boys," he began, "you are more man than any Raider, for you fight to save your sisters and mothers. And save them we will. When you are old, you will tell your grandchildren of this day."

Ivar stopped fighting, and the boys holding him slowly eased back. There was a dark stain on his trousers—he'd lost control of his bladder. Ivar saw Otec notice. Knowing such a thing could haunt the boy for the rest of his life, Otec said, "Fear touches all men. It's what you do with that fear that counts." He said it loud enough and with enough conviction for all the boys to hear. Hands shaking, Ivar took up his bow and settled back into position.

Moments later, Otec heard the sound of marching. He peered over the trees stripped of their leaves, to the canyon floor, stained black and choked with still-smoking debris. Orange flames glowed here and there whenever the wind picked up.

The Raiders came into the open as they rounded the tip of the mountain row by row. The cadence of their marching feet reminded Otec of the sound of drums in the distance.

When the last of the Raiders were directly in front of Otec and his company of boys, Hargar strode to the top of the black-ened rise, his feet kicking up clouds of ash. A chill wind tugged at his cloak. He appeared a lone man facing five hundred Raiders. "I mark you for the dead. By my axe, I swear you shall never see your home shores again. I will throw your broken bones into the rivers, and they will be food for the fishes."

There was a murmur of derision among the Raiders, and some of the soldiers in front drew their twin blades.

Hargar simply waited, his axe and shield by his sides. One of the Raider commanders gave an order. A note rang out on an instrument that was part flute, part whistle, and the soldiers formed into a phalanx. Another note and they charged the hill. Hargar waited until they were halfway up, and then he gave a great shout.

At the signal, all the boys on the mountain stood. Working tirelessly over the last few days, the Tyron and Argon women had increased their arrows by double, though some of them didn't fly true. Thirty arrows for each boy. "Make sure each one counts!" Otec called out.

He took three arrows in his hand at once, aiming and firing as quickly as he could. As the arrows struck true, the Raiders milled in confusion. When the flute blew out another melody, two companies split off. The men in the center put away their swords, pulled out recurve bows, and aimed for Otec and his boys.

"Take cover!" Otec cried.

The boys ducked behind rocks or simply lay flat. But they had the high ground, leaving the Raiders a very small angle to hit any of them.

When the first volley flagged, Otec grabbed three arrows and loosed them one right after another, then crouched down, grabbed three more, and shot those. It wasn't long before all of the boys were doing the same.

Otec spared a glance at the clashing armies. His father, too, had the high ground. And swords weren't much good at blocking the heft of an axe swing.

The flute-like instrument called out again. Another company of Raiders split off, charging up the mountain toward Otec's group. They splashed through the crystal-clear waters of the Shyle River and penetrated the bare-branched forest.

Otec peered down at them, his cold fingers gripping the gritty outcropping of rock. They would kill his boys—the boys he'd sworn to keep safe. But he could not order them to run, for if he did, the Raiders would surely overwhelm his father and the other clansmen.

Otec's gaze swept up the mountain, pausing on both sides of the shelf where his boys stood. The Raiders would have to climb a narrow, steep path to reach them. And they would have to go through him to touch any of them.

He pushed his arrows into another of the boy's hands—one of the twins. Suddenly he knew which one. "Ake, if I fall, you order the boys to climb the mountain and disappear."

The boy nodded wordlessly. Otec gave his hand a squeeze of solidarity and luck, then picked up his borrowed axe and shield. This time, the weight felt right in his hands. He positioned himself at the best place in the path, where it was so narrow only one man at a time could approach. He thought of all the times he'd defended his flock from a bear or wolves. This was no different.

The first man burst through, his face flushed with cold and blackened with soot. Otec blocked the Raider's thrust with his shield and chopped with the axe. The man fell, and within seconds his life's blood ran down the channels carved into the mountains by decades of rainwater.

Another man charged, but Otec blocked him effortlessly. As the Raider twisted his blades and danced his fancy footwork, Otec blocked again and chopped. Blocked and chopped until the Raider fell.

Two men charged Otec next. He blocked one, but the other arced his sword down, slicing into Otec's arm. He felt no pain.

He bashed one of the men with the rim of his shield, shoving him back. The Raider stumbled, then toppled end over end out of sight. Suddenly, another man appeared and swung at Otec, but this Raider also stumbled back, an arrow sticking from his throat, blood gurgling from his mouth. Otec glanced up to see Ivar watching him. They shared a nod.

The boys ran out of arrows and stood at the edge of the shelf, using stones and slings to decimate the company charged with murdering them. Otec fought on until the seemingly never-ending stream of Raiders dried up. He glanced up at the rock shelf—at the boys cheering, their bows raised above their heads.

Otec studied the battlefield below but couldn't tell which army was winning. Although the clanmen held the high ground and fought ferociously, they were still greatly outnumbered. He looked up at the boys, pride swelling within him.

"When you woke this morning, you were all boys," Otec called out. "When you lie down tonight, you will lie down as men. But I will ask one thing more of you. If we hit the Raider's flank, we can turn the tide of this battle. We can ensure victory for our fathers and brothers."

He waited as the boys looked at each other. "If you will lead us, Otec," Ivar said. "We will go."

"Then take your axes and shields, my men, and we will end this battle."

Otec took his group of men and slipped silently down the mountain. They gathered in a line, the fear in their eyes eclipsed by a quiet confidence. Otec gave the signal and they rushed forward, ramming into the enemy's flank. The Raiders barely had time to shift their focus before Otec and his men fell on them.

The clanmen saw their boys and gave a great shout, exploding through the line. The tide of the battle shifted, the clanmen now holding the edge. A few minutes later, Otec took a swing, finishing the Raider before him. And then he saw Jore. If Jore was alive, what had happened to Matka? Then Otec realized Jore was fighting Hargar, his father. For the first time, fear penetrated the haze of battle that had taken hold of Otec. He had seen Jore fight, noticed the skill and experience with which this Raider wielded his blades.

Otec was running toward Jore almost before he'd even thought to do it. His axe arced hard and fast. But then Jore dropped to his knees, his swords crossing under Hargar's shield and slashing across his midsection.

Matka had called Otec innocent. That innocence burnt away in a moment, leaving righteous fury. He arced his axe down with all his strength. Jore barely had time to dive to the side. Otec was already shifting his momentum, his shield slamming into the Raider and sending him flying.

Jore hadn't even landed before Otec was on him, swinging his axe hard. But the other man's experience served him well. Lightning fast, his foot flicked up, kicking Otec's leg. His leg cramped up and his attack faltered, giving enough time for Jore to gain his feet and launch his own attack.

Ducking behind his shield, Otec sured up his shield with his axe head. He peered out from behind the shield and used it to deflect one of Jore's swords, then slammed his axe into the man's knee, buckling it. Otec pulled his axe free of Jore's bones and swung again. The axe blade bit deep into the Raider's side, and he fell, his eyes wide.

Staggering with exhaustion, Otec glanced around to make sure no one was coming after him, but most of the Idarans were already dead. A flake of snow landed on his cheek and immediately melted, running down like a tear. He absently wiped it away as he turned to search for his father.

He found him, amid the dead and injured. Hargar lay quietly on his back, his feet propped up on the back of a dead Immortal. Otec rushed to his side and took one of his hands. Hargar was soaked in blood from his stomach down. He looked into Otec's eyes, profound sadness making his gaze heavy. "Your mother is here."

Otec whipped his head around, but she was nowhere to be seen. His father must be hallucinating.

Hargar groaned and shifted, his expression pained. "She's come to take me with her to the dead. And I will gladly go."

A wave of horror washed through Otec at the realization that his mother was dead. "No, Father. Please. I can't face this by myself."

With great effort, Hargar rested his hand on Otec's shoulder. "You are the clan chief now. You have responsibilities, and you will not shirk them. You will grow into the man the Shyle needs you to be. You will lead them away from these dark times and into the light."

Tears poured down Otec's face. "What if there isn't a clan left?"

Hargar's mouth tightened and he winced. "Our people are strong. Strong as stone and supple as a sapling. They will not break. Not ever."

Otec slowly nodded. Hargar took hold of his axe, passing it to Otec's hands. "Take my axe and shield and use them to defend our people."

He took them, feeling the smooth polished wood, noting the notches in the shield. "I will, Father."

Hargar closed his eyes and let out a long breath. He did not draw another.

Otec reached into his pocket and drew out the little mouse with the broken ear and too-big eyes. With one small chop of his axe, it was only a broken, insignificant piece of wood. Otec staggered away from the crushed carving. Away from the father he feared he would never be good enough for.

"She's still alive," a raspy voice called. Startled, Otec looked down the hill to see Jore watching him. "One does not simply kill a priestess," the mortally injured Raider continued, "not if you don't want to incur the wrath of the Goddess. If you hurry, you could save her."

The day they'd left the Shyle, Jore had told Otec to remember, because the Raider had known his village was about to be attacked. Otec stumbled toward the Raider, barely restraining himself from finishing Jore off. "Where is she?"

Jore expression began to relax. "All I know is they left her behind in the village. They couldn't kill her, but the elements could."

After making sure no weapons were within arm's reach, Otec crouched near Jore and asked, "Why didn't you stop them?"

"If I had tried, they would have killed me."

"What about my family?"

"There are a hundred guards."

Otec turned to move away, but Jore's hand flashed out, grabbing his arm. "Tell her . . . tell her I'm sorry."

This was the man who had killed Otec's father and abandoned his own sister. "You followed the darkness," Otec said. "There is no excuse for that."

Stillness began to steal over Jore's face. His breaths grew deeper. Otec turned and walked away. Some people deserved to die alone, with no one to mourn them.

13

O tec stood at the top of the rise, numb beyond seeing blood and death. Beyond seeing anything but the blinding whiteness. He wondered if this was what Matka meant when she said he was innocent. "Ignorant" was perhaps a better word, since he had certainly been ignorant to suffering and pain. But he was not anymore.

He held his father's axe and shield in his hand, felt the comforting weight of them grounding his entire body. His feet ached as he stood in a hand span of snow. He turned to look out over the men wandering among the dead and injured. There were women too, by the hundreds. They loaded up the injured to take them back to the villages to be cared for. And they wept over their dead.

Seneth came to stand beside him. "You must take your father's place."

Otec breathed in, the cold air knifing through his lungs. "How? They are my father's men. My brother's men."

"Then you must make them yours."

Otec scoffed. "I don't have the experience or knowledge to lead them."

"What I heard from Ivar was a far different story." Seneth took hold of Otec's arm. "You're bleeding." He motioned to someone.

"It's not deep," Otec protested.

"Still, it is best to care for it before it becomes infected," Narium said as she eased up beside him. She washed the wound with something that smelled of garlic, then wrapped it with boiled rags, her hands warm against his chilled skin.

"Anything else?" she asked gently.

He started to shake his head, but Seneth said, "He's limping. Right leg."

"It's just bruised," Otec said.

Narium bent down, her pregnant belly nearly making her lose her balance. Otec steadied her. "Go look after someone who really needs it. I'll be fine."

Her eyes filled with compassion and she opened her mouth.

"I can't talk about it," Otec cut her off before she could say anything about his father's death. Such kindness might crack the thin ice shielding him from the black river of emotions churning within him.

Narium gave him a small smile, then waddled away. Otec turned to find Seneth staring at the sky. "That is a strange bird."

Otec followed his friend's gaze. The white owl circled above their heads. It hovered before Otec, hooting with some kind of urgency, before turning and flying back the way it had come. "It isn't a bird," he said firmly. He needed to hurry if he was going to save Matka.

Undon hiked toward them, his red beard a strange contrast to his blond hair. "We've made the final count—only four hundred or so Raiders are accounted for."

"Then the rest are still in the Shyle," Otec said.

"How do you know?" Seneth asked.

"Raiders take slaves." Otec called Ivar over and said, "Gather up anyone strong enough to fight. If we hurry, we can reach the village before morning." The boy took off at a run.

Undon looked toward Shyleholm and back at him again. "My men have marched hard for three days and battled today. They need rest."

"We can still fight." Otec turned to find the clanmen gathering behind him, their breaths leaving their bodies in clouds of white that seemed to ring them on all sides. The blood on their clothing had frozen stiff.

"I'm with Undon," said a Shyle clanman named Destin. He was about thirty years old, with pox scars on both cheeks. "We can't run blind into another battle. We need to scout out Shyleholm. Attack when we're fresh."

Otec gritted his teeth. "What do you think the Raiders will do when they find out we've defeated the rest of them? We cannot take that risk with our families—we cannot abandon them for even a day."

The wind tugged on Undon's thinning blond hair. "I will not risk my men. They're too exhausted to fight. Besides, I have a few prisoners to interrogate. I'm hoping to have some new information to pass on to High Chief Burdin."

The winter wind whipped along Otec's body, but his shiver came from a sense of foreboding. "Undon, we need you."

The man shook his head. "You'll have to do without." He motioned to his men and they separated themselves and began moving away.

Otec watched them go, their passing kicking up the white snow to reveal black ash beneath.

"We'll wait for tomorrow," Destin said as his pale-blue eyes looked for support from the group of Argons and Shyle. "Then perhaps the Tyrons will be ready to go with us."

Otec looked at his fellow clanmen, who were already starting to back away. "Sometimes you don't have time to make plans and rest. You just have to move." But they weren't listening.

Seneth clapped a hand on his shoulder. "I agree," he said loudly. "And the Argons will fight beside you."

Otec closed his eyes in relief, feeling the snow melting against his cheeks, washing away the ash that coated his skin. He gave Seneth a subtle nod of gratitude.

Seneth motioned to his men. "Round up the horses. Let's go."

Otec glanced down to find Destin glaring at him. "Shyle, move out." Otec pushed through the crowd, not checking to see if they would follow, but hoping against hope that they would.

He heard footsteps following him, but didn't dare look back until he reached the horses hidden in a box canyon. All the men were there. Even Destin, who paused beside him. "This doesn't have to be a fight. Step down and let someone with more experience take over."

Otec tightened the cinch on his horse's saddle a bit more forcefully than necessary. "Someone like you?"

Destin shrugged his wiry shoulders. "I fought beside your brothers. Fought under your father. That's more than you can say." He turned away to find his own horse.

Otec watched him go as the wind picked up, blowing with sharpness through the spaces of his coat. He closed his eyes, rested his forehead against the saddle, and took in the familiar smells of horse and leather.

"Otec?" He looked up to see Seneth already mounted, looking down at him.

He took a deep breath of the biting wind and swung up into the saddle. They rode through the dark night, sticking to the road so the horses didn't trip over their own feet in the rising snow.

In the gray light of morning, Otec ordered his men to surround their own village. Pushing through snow that reached the middle of his shins, he took in his home. He couldn't help but think of Matka's drawing of a cozy village brimming with life and comfort. Now many of the homes were burned-out ruins. The air still carried the acrid smell of burning, and tendrils of smoke rose from deep within the partially collapsed walls.

Otec moved into position, catching glimpses inside old lady Bothilda's house, of her spinning wheel, still set up with wool from the spring shearing. As he passed the open door at the back of the house, a raven started and took flight. Otec glanced inside and realized the bird had been eating the old woman's cat. One side of the cat was blackened to a crisp, the other side untouched. The cat's eyes were missing.

A minute later, Otec took up position behind his clan house. Part of the roof had burned, but most of the building was still intact. The owl appeared again, hooting and flying out of sight behind the barn. For now, Otec didn't follow it. He had to get inside the clan house, search for his family first.

When the signal came that the last man was in place, the clanmen darted out of hiding, silent as they slipped inside the houses to kill the Raiders sleeping in their stolen beds.

Readjusting his sweaty grip on his axe, Otec pushed open the clan-house door. The place smelled of days-old ashes. He wandered from one room to another, a breathless hope that he would find all of them inside. A burning dread that they would be dead. But in the end, all he was left with was hollow confusion. The house was empty.

Otec stumbled back into the early morning light and saw his men wandering around, clearly as bewildered as he was. Some were running, calling their loved ones' names. There was no one. Even Otec's dog was gone.

Seneth came jogging up to him. "The village has been abandoned. There are no Raiders or Shyle anywhere."

"Where could they have gone?" Otec turned in a circle, hoping to see even one of the women. "They have to be here somewhere. Search every building. Send men out to the summer homes. Surely some of them escaped there."

Otec looked around for the owl, but it was nowhere in sight. The snow came harder now. He hiked his coat up higher on his shoulders, his body shivering with exhaustion, cold, and hunger. He wasn't sure how much longer he could force himself to go before he collapsed. He only knew that moment was not yet upon him.

Steeling himself, he checked the barn. Thistle and all the horses were gone. Otec exited at the back of the barn and squinted into the distance. To the west of the village, dark figures moved through the snowy fields. Judging by their size, they had to be women.

He started toward them, passing the old meat shed. But his foot slipped on a patch of ice hidden beneath the snow. He could have sworn it wasn't there when he'd placed his foot. He lay still for a few moment, trying to dredge up the energy to force his body up.

The owl was sitting on the meat shed, staring at him. His backside aching, Otec rolled to the side and pushed himself up when he noticed the shed door had been opened since the snow had begun to fall.

His eyes lifted to the owl even as he strode forward and yanked on the door. But it was locked. With one swing of his axe, Otec broke through the old wood. Inside the barn, Matka hung by her hands from a rusted meat hook. Her clothes were torn and bloody, her exposed skin bruised and mottled with cold. Her head hung down, her normally dark skin as gray as ash-covered snow.

Otec rushed over and lifted her, but he couldn't untie the knot around the meat hook. "I need help! I need help in here!"

There were running footsteps, and then the Argons came. Otec held Matka as they cut through the ropes. She collapsed into his arms, her body lifeless. He hauled her outside and gently set her down in the clean snow.

She looked dead. Her eyes were sunken into her skull, her bones sticking out. They must not have fed her at all in the days since he'd seen her last.

Otec held her face close to his. "Matka? Can you hear me?" No response.

Sharina, one of his mother's assistant healers and friends, bustled over, her eyes wide.

"Where did you come from?" Otec asked in surprise, his voice breathless with hope.

Sharina knelt and pressed her ear to Matka's mouth. "When they attacked the village, some of us escaped into the forest. The Raiders left yesterday morning through Shyle Pass. They took hundreds of villagers with them."

That would have been right after Otec's men had ambushed the Raiders. "Were any of my family with you?" he asked.

Sharina shook her head. "The Raiders took them out first."

Otec had to fight to keep his dark emotions locked tight away. He stared toward the mountains he could barely see through the blinding snow. "We have to go after them."

Seneth followed his gaze. "We push the men any harder, and they'll start dying. Let them have one night of warmth, rest, and food. Then we'll go after them together."

"Who is she?" Seneth asked as he gestured toward Matka.

Sharina's gaze locked with Otec's, silent communication passing between them. "She's a highwoman," Otec said without hesitation. "The Idarans took her as a slave. But she managed to escape, only to find herself their captive again. And all to save a handful of clanmen."

Sharina rested her palm on the girl's chest. "She's breathing. Her heart beats, but weakly. You must get her warm. It's all any of us can do for her." She pushed to her feet. "And now I'm going to go see if I can help anyone else."

With Seneth's aid, Otec lifted Matka into his arms. Her head came to rest against his chest. "I promised Holla I'd look after you." The words nearly broke him. But he held himself together. He still had his family to save. "Please don't die."

Seneth stepped back, his penetrating gaze on Otec. "You care for her," the older man said. When Otec didn't deny it, Seneth offered, "I'll handle everything tonight."

Otec nodded gratefully and trudged through the snow to the hollow clan house.

"But Otec?"

He paused and looked back at Seneth.

"Tomorrow, you'll have to be the clan chief again."

"Yes." Otec paused. "Stay in the Bends' house. It looks intact and has enough room."

In the clan-house kitchen, Otec lit a fire and built it up until it roared, then placed Matka as close to it as he dared. He shut the door to the great hall and stuffed blankets from the bedrooms under the door. He washed Matka's face and hands with hot water and an extra blanket, then wrapped her in his own furs.

In the cellar, he stepped carefully over broken pots of dried herbs and righted barrels empty of the apples that should have seen his family through the winter. He ate some cheese he'd found under a tipped-over stool. Matka started to shiver, so he made some hot tea and got her to swallow some. Her color seemed better after that.

Despite the eerie silence, Otec couldn't keep his eyes open any longer. He lay down beside Matka and curled around her shivering body to comfort himself and warm her. He fell quickly asleep.

When he awoke later, his whole body was stiff and aching. It was still dark out. He sat up to see Matka staring at the ceiling, her hands clutching the furs spread over both of their bodies. Her vacant expression nearly destroyed him. He didn't think he could bear it if the Raiders had broken her mind.

"Matka?" he said hesitantly.

"They took Holla," she replied in a monotone, her expression frozen in place. "They took all of them."

Otec reached over her to toss more logs into the embers. "They were alive?"

Matka didn't respond at first. "Your mother died fighting them. But the rest, yes."

His father had been right. "What did they do with her body?"

"They burned them," Matka said softly. "It's how the Idarans deal with all their dead."

A sob hitched in Otec's throat. The ice encasing his emotions shattered at once, flooding him with such grief he couldn't bear it. Matka held his hand until Otec managed to swallow his sobs and ask, "Why did they leave you behind?"

She stared at the ceiling. "Tyleze threw me in with the clan. They would have killed me. But Holla wouldn't let them. When Tyleze came for my body and found me alive instead, he hauled me into the meat shed." Her whole body trembled as if the memories were trying to break their way out of her skin.

"Because despite all they had done to me, they dared not kill me and they dared not take me with them. They knew if they did, I'd find a way to kill them. And they were right." Matka let out a shaky breath. "So they decided to leave me in the cold, to let the Goddess of Winter finish me off."

A single tear rolled down her bruised cheek. "Jore is dead, isn't he?" Otec could only nod. She closed her eyes, biting her bottom lip. "I knew when I woke up and saw you instead of him that he was gone."

"I'm sorry."

She had no idea how sorry Otec was, but he couldn't tell her he'd killed her brother. She'd hate him for it, and he couldn't bear that.

Matka pressed the heels of her hands into her eyes and sobbed. Now it was Otec's turn to comfort her. When she'd calmed down, he found a pot of grains on one of the shelves and made them some gruel and fried pork belly.

Then they slept again.

14

Otec woke before dawn and began to gather his winter gear. He stepped into the kitchen to find Matka standing with her back to him before a bowl of steaming water, a soapy rag in her hand. He got a good look at the bloody welts criss-crossing her back before she shoved her arms into her tattered tunic and pulled it over her shoulders.

Feeling the urge to kill whatever man had done that to her, Otec dumped his gear by one of the chairs and began the arduous task of putting it on. "Take whatever you need," he told Matka. "I'll be back as soon as I can."

She dropped the rag in the water with a splash. "I'm coming with you."

"Matka—"

"It's my fault!" She braced herself against the table. "If I hadn't trusted Tyleze, if I would have warned your family, the village could have fled in the night. Or maybe someone could have gone for help. Something . . ."

Otec studied this woman, took in her betrayal—consciously done or not—and was surprised he had only compassion for her. Would she feel the same if she knew he had killed her brother? For the briefest moment, he considered telling her. But what good would it do? Jore was dead. Otec's father was dead. Nothing could change that. Telling Matka would only increase her pain.

Otec determined then that it was a burden he would bear alone. He reached out, taking her hand. "If I would have stayed, maybe I could have helped them get away. Or I could have died in the attack." He shook his head, desperately wanting her to understand what he couldn't say. "We have to let this go."

"I'm coming with you," she said firmly. "If I slow you down, you can leave me behind."

Otec studied her haunted expression and realized she would never forgive herself if she didn't do this. "All right. Finish washing your wounds—Mother always said that was important to preventing blood poisoning." He stumbled back from the table that was still sticky and smelled like apples.

He paused before the door to tie on his snowshoes. "Take what you need and try to find us some more food. I'll be back for you."

Matka nodded wordlessly.

Otec stepped out into a full-on blizzard and made his way to the Bends' house—it was one of the few that still seemed perfectly intact. He opened the door to find the floor covered with a mixture of Argon and Shyle clanmen sleeping in neat rows and columns. "Up!" he called to them. "Go through all the houses and find winter gear and food. We're leaving at daybreak." The men hauled themselves to their feet.

Pushing pale blond hair out of his face, Destin shot Otec a disapproving look. But with nothing to argue about, he gathered up his things and went with the others.

Seneth watched Otec from his place beside the fire. Judging by his bloodshot eyes, Seneth hadn't slept yet. Otec made his way toward him, when someone shouted his name.

"Dobber?" Otec said.

The other man enveloped Otec in a hug. "You're alive, Dobber! How?" He'd thought all the men in the Shyle at the time of the Raiders' attack were dead.

Dobber pushed back, tears pooling in his eyes. "My father and I tried to fight them off. When I woke up, my house was burning and it was over. All I could do was hide."

"What about your family?"

Dobber shook his head. "My father is dead. The rest were taken."

Otec squeezed his shoulders. "We'll get them back."

After a moment, Dobber nodded wordlessly.

"Go into my family's meat shed," Otec said. "See if you can find any food the Raiders left behind."

Dobber turned to go.

Seneth motioned Otec over to the fire and said, "Dozens of your women escaped into the forests. Most fled to the summer homes higher up the mountains. There's no way of knowing for sure how many until the storm breaks."

Otec sank into a chair. Already he was feeling too hot in his winter gear. "And the Raiders?"

Seneth leaned forward. "The story I've pieced together is that they fled with their captives as soon as we defeated the Idarans in the pass, though I'm not sure how they knew."

Otec studied the storm through the bubbled glass of a small window. "We'll catch up to them."

Seneth tossed a log onto the embers, then prodded it with a stick to get it to start up again, but the wood was wet and stubborn. "Otec, our orders were to stop the threat to our northern borders. After that, we were to return and support the cities still under attack."

Otec blinked at Seneth, not believing what he was hearing. "You want us to abandon our women and children to them?"

Seneth blew out through his nose. "They started up yesterday just after daybreak. They took all the horses and wagons, so they were probably moving pretty fast. The storm came from the south, so if they beat it over the summit, they're probably safely on the other side. And if they didn't . . ."

"They're trapped in this storm," Otec finished for him.

"And right now, the snow's too deep for the horses to break through. Your only option to go after them is snowshoes." Seneth's eyes were full of compassion. "What's on the other side of the pass, Otec?"

Otec watched the steam sizzling out of the log that refused to burn. He'd traveled Shyle Pass with the sheep before, but never beyond. "The sheer cliffs of Darbenmore . . . the only ones who can navigate those cliffs are Darbens." The Darbens had built their village into recessions in the cliffs. They were a solitary lot, living off the sea and a few crops they grew on the mountainsides.

"And apparently very, very desperate Raiders," Seneth said darkly. He poked the stubborn log again.

Otec closed his eyes and spoke low. "Seneth, I don't know if the Shyle will follow me without your support."

Seneth tossed away the poker, which clattered loudly on the floor. "I can't risk my family's safety any more than you can. If the clan lands fall, so will they."

Otec stared at the smoking piece of wood. "Destin already told me he'd do a better job of leading."

Seneth grunted. "Had it been up to him, we would have spent the night freezing in the middle of the canyon and you would be another day behind your women and children."

Otec watched the log finally catch fire. "Go, Seneth. Your place is defending your family. As is mine."

Seneth lifted haunted eyes. "I'm sorry."

Otec rose to his feet, sweat building up under his clothing. "I have a hundred clanmen, more than enough on my own. Know that the Shyle will always be in your debt. A debt we will repay if ever you need us."

He turned around before the other man could see the emotions in his face, then stepped outside and helped his men find gear and food. When they had finished, the sun was cresting the mountaintops.

Otec looked his men over. They wore mismatched gear and bedrolls packed with supplies. But their faces were determined. Dobber nodded to him.

Otec nodded back and then headed toward the front of the Shyle men. They watched him warily. But no one argued or tried to usurp him.

Someone touched his arm and he turned to find Ivar and the twins behind him. "We're going with you."

Otec shot a look back at Seneth, who merely waved him on. "They insisted," he called, smiling. "I think they're more your men than mine now."

Otec nodded. Though they were just boys, he was grateful to at least have some allies.

He didn't have to fetch Matka. She was already waiting for him in front of the clan house doors, her swords gleaming silver at her back. Grumbles turned to shouts of outrage.

Destin started past Otec, but he grabbed the man's arm. "She was their slave," he said firmly. "She did not know of their plans. And she saved me from them so that I might warn everyone."

Destin glared at him. "She was the one writing that book—doesn't sound like a slave to me."

Otec studied the men behind him, saw their hatred, and knew that they did not believe him. "Show them your back," he said.

Matka's gaze shot to him, anger and humiliation flashing in turns across her face. But she dropped her swords and bedroll. Then her coat. Then she turned and lifted her shirt, exposing the cuts and bruises across her skin.

"By the Balance," Ivar said.

Shivering, Matka shoved her shirt down and turned to face the men, her clothes already laced with snow. "They killed my mother and my sister. If I can, I will spare you my fate."

"Wasn't one of them your brother?" Destin said, but the heat was gone from his voice.

"He was the one who did that to me," she answered.

"You could have fought your way free," he pointed out. "It's not like you were never alone."

"They would have killed my other sister if I'd rebelled—she's still in Idara." That wasn't exactly true, but Otec knew she couldn't tell the clanmen she was hoping the Raiders had changed their minds.

Destin hesitated before stepping forward, picking up her coat off the ground, and handing it to her. "You could have told us at any time, and we would have helped you."

"I believe that now." Matka looked at Otec as she said this. She pushed her arms into the coat and fixed the toggles at the front.

Otec handed her the bedroll and swords. "Are you sure you're up for this? Yesterday you were nearly dead."

She glanced up as the owl passed overhead. "You don't need to worry. They're not done with me yet."

She strode away. He watched her, shivering as he remembered his curse and the fairy's promise.

They crossed the summit just before nightfall and descended rapidly. Just before full dark, Otec found what he'd been looking for—a cave. It was occupied. But even a bear didn't stand much chance against a hundred clanmen.

In the cave, which seemed to be made of columns of receding rock, they roasted bear meat over a roaring fire. No one spoke much. Otec lay down next to Ivar and the twins, who immediately fell asleep.

The ground was full of rocks. Otec could normally sleep anywhere, but he couldn't stop worrying about his family. He even wondered what had happened to his dog, Freckles, and then decided he'd rather not know. He didn't miss Thistle, though. If the Raiders stole her, they were at the losing end of the bargain.

He finally gave up and went to the cave mouth. Matka was there, the light from the small fire she'd lit highlighting the planes of her face as she chewed on her nails. Otec sat beside her.

"On summer nights," she whispered, "the nights are shadow upon shadow. But in the winter, the snow changes everything, reflecting the silver moonlight. Instead of shades of evergreen and slate, the hue is the blue-gray of smoke. I wish I had my charcoals."

Otec watched her hands twitch and knew the itch to create something was just under her skin. "The fairy—how long has it been following you?"

"Do not say it out loud!" she whispered harshly.

He scooted closer. "She already knows you can see her."

Matka drew in a ragged breath. "How do you—"

"She spoke to me."

"What?" Matka gasped. Her head whipped around, but her face was cast in shadow so Otec couldn't see her expression. "But men never see them!"

Jerking his head toward the sleeping clanmen, he shushed her. She nodded and leaned toward her small fire, motioning for him to come closer. "They don't like smoke."

"Why?"

She looked away, fiddling with a torn fingernail. "She's been following me since I was a child, but she never spoke to me before the night she warned me that Immortals were near."

Otec sat back. "So that's how you knew the Raiders were there." She nodded. "And the fires—the luminash?"

Matka tore off a piece of her fingernail and spit it into the fire before starting on another one. "I asked her for help—I knew I'd never get you free otherwise."

"But I thought you said they were tricksy and cruel?"

In a jerky motion, Matka bit off another piece of nail, this time drawing blood. She didn't seem to notice. "I made them a deal."

Otec leaned forward, taking her arm in his hand. "What? What is it?"

She wiped the blood onto her furs, then sat on her hands. "It doesn't matter. It's done now, and it won't come to pass anyway. I'll make sure of that."

His brow furrowed. "What won't come to pass?"

She shook him off and rose to her feet. "It doesn't matter." She lifted up the edge of her blankets and climbed inside.

He watched her turn her back to him. "Matka, could they help us save my family?"

She glanced back at him, the light from the fire casting dark hollows under her eyes. "I have nothing left to bargain with. They've taken everything I have." She rolled back over, tugging the furs over her head.

"What about me?" Otec asked softly. "What can I offer them?"

"There's nothing more they want from you," came the muffled response from under the blankets.

"Do you swear it?"

"I do," she answered.

He believed her. He wanted to go to her, to hold her as he had that night at the clan house. But judging by the stiff set of her shoulders, she wouldn't let him.

15

At first light, the company of Shyle clanmen continued down the pass. With the sun came warmth, which softened the snow into slush that quickly turned to mud. Without fresh snow to cover the tracks, evidence of their families and their captors became more abundant. Otec froze at the sight of a half-buried piece of wood. He wouldn't have noticed it at all, except for the familiar blond color of fresh wood.

He crouched down and pulled the carving from the sticky mud. Then he took a bit of snow from the shade under a bush and scrubbed the white crystals across the ruined surface.

It was a beaver—the beaver he'd carved for Holla. Split exactly down the middle, the edges too cleanly cut to have been made by anything but a blade. Otec's eyes darted around, looking for any signs of blood.

"Something happened here. Something bad," he murmured to Matka as she knelt beside him. He took a deep breath and thought he could smell fish and smoke on the breeze. He rose, his knees cracking, to face his clanmen. "If the Raiders manage to escape across the sea, they'll be beyond our reach. Come on."

Otec started off at a trot with Matka at his side, the men falling in behind them. They must have kept up that pace for an hour when he saw the smoke, billowing in a black, churning mass.

Finally, they reached the end of the pass and saw the basalt cliffs, which appeared to be made up of hundreds of columns rising vertically out of the sea. A cruel breeze blew off the choppy, dark waters. About half a league to the west, Otec saw the city of Darben.

Gasping for breath and pressing the heel of his hand into the ache in his side, he followed the pillar of smoke rising in the east. He stepped closer to the edge of the steep cliffs. A third of a league away was a village that had been built into a shelf of rock, about halfway between the cliff-top and the beach.

"Matka, bring out your telescope," he called. She did so and peered through it as he squinted into the distance, trying to make out what was going on through the haze of smoke.

"Down on the beach," she said breathlessly. "The Idarans are fighting with the Darbens."

"Our families!" Destin cried. "Are they there? Are they safe?"

"Yes!" she said. "Bound and gagged. The Idarans are forcing them into the boats."

Otec took off running, the rest of the clanmen right on his heels. Moving along the edge of the mountain that broke off abruptly into cliffs, they scattered an odd mixture of animals—sheep, goats, cattle, horses, and even a donkey. And then Otec recognized the donkey—Thistle. The Raiders had taken the animals they'd wanted and abandoned the rest.

Otec heard it first, the screams and shouts of battle, followed by the sound of knives and blades doing their dark work. "Ivar, Ake, and Arvid, stay in the back!" he hollered without turning to look for them.

They reached an archway at the head of a narrow flight of stairs that had been carved into the sides of the cliffs, with nothing but air between the men and the abrupt drop-off. About halfway down was the village of Darbenmore.

Coughing at the smoke billowing into his face, Otec took out his axe and shield and rushed down the zigzagging stairs. He charged headlong into the wide shelf the village had been built upon. The houses were made of wood, and most were burning, pyres for the dead he could see turning to ash inside. He shot past the first house, the heat reaching out with fat, greedy fingers to singe his hair and blast heat against his skin.

Standing in the center of the main path was a woman. She screamed at the sight of the clanmen, soot mixing with the tears streaming down her face. The men simply parted around her while she continued screaming.

On the other side of the village were more stairs. The clanmen started down, and without the smoke to block the view, Otec felt dizzy at the sharp drop-off. Below, fewer than fifty Darben men were retreating toward the stairs. When they saw the clanmen they backed off, coming to a stop at the bottom of the cliffs.

The Idarans saw the clanmen too, and boats loaded with stolen cargo began pulling away.

Otec was the first one off the stairs. "Free them or they're lost to us forever!"

His men charged forward onto the docks, anger giving them power. Otec launched himself at a Raider who was trying to force one of the older women—by the Balance, it was Enrid!—onto a boat. Otec cut him down before he could even turn.

With a swing of his shield, Otec bashed another man's face in. He passed Enrid his knife and she immediately set about freeing herself and the children.

Otec ducked a jab from a Raider, using his shield to block the other blade. Then he drove his axe through an opening in the man's guard, hitting him square in the chest. The man fell and did not rise again.

Otec lunged toward another Raider when he heard a scuffle directly behind him. He whipped back around and saw that Enrid had launched herself onto the back of a Raider who must've been about to kill Otec. With a primal scream, she drove her knife into his side.

Otec pivoted, his axe arcing toward the man and connecting with his chest. Still screaming, the Raider staggered back and landed with Enrid in the freezing black water.

"Enrid!" Otec cried. The Shyle didn't know how to swim, and even if they did, their heavy winter clothes would drag them down. He stepped to the edge of the dock and saw dozens of women and children in the water, heads bobbing, mouths gasping. None of them made a sound. Otec jerked off his coat, preparing to go after them, but long poles appeared in front of him.

The men of Darben were lowering long fishing spears, butt first, into the water, drawing the Shyle safely to shore. Choking and sputtering, Enrid held onto a pole.

Otec whipped around, looking for another Raider to kill. But they were all dead. He scanned quickly and found the Argon boys near the back of the docks.

Other clanmen lay belly first, fishing more people out of the water. Otec was just about to help them when he heard someone shout his name.

Pushing his way to the end of the dock, he stared at the boats already in the water, white sails unfurling. His gaze raked over them. Some were nearly full of Raiders who had obviously abandoned their slaves in favor of surviving. Others were loaded with Otec's people. "Holla, Storm, Wesson, Aldi, Eira, Magnhild, Bothilda, Helka!"

A half dozen voices rose up to answer—he recognized them instantly. He whipped around and saw them. His family. His younger brothers and all his sisters stuffed in a boat, so close he could make out all the details of their faces. It was Holla screaming for him, reaching out even as Storm held her down.

Otec grabbed fistfuls of his hair, not knowing what to do or how to reach them. The remaining boats were sunk or drifting, and he had no idea how to operate one even if they were usable. Determined to reach them one way or another, he stripped off his coat and was starting on his boots when Dobber grabbed his arms. "You can't swim!"

Otec tried to shrug him off. "It doesn't matter."

Matka darted in front of him, her hand up. "Stop!"

"I have to save them! I have to!"

She grabbed his shirt in her fist. "We will. We'll go after them. I swear it, but jumping in that water will only get you killed."

Knowing she was right, Otec called out to his family, "I'll come for you! I won't give up!" His gaze went to the other boats—the ones with only Raiders inside. He drew his bow from his back. "Clanmen, we're going to need those boats."

His men lined up beside him, drew back their bows, and cleared the stolen boats of vermin. When they were drifting, Otec shifted his gaze to the boats moving out to sea. He watched Storm disappear from view.

Otec turned to face his clanmen. Many of them were crying and holding their wives and children in relief. With a quick count, he realized that nearly one hundred of their clan members had been saved. Watching their joy through the lens of his own loss, Otec felt as though his heart was being encased by ice.

"Dobber!" one of the men cried. Otec watched as a woman was pulled from the water, her face pale as death. Coughing wetly, she reached for Dobber, who cried out and ran toward her. She was his mother, the only family he had left.

Otec straightened his shoulders and marched toward the men of Darbenmore. "I need those boats. And I need people who can operate them."

A man stepped forward. "I will help you, clanman. They killed my wife and daughter, but you saved my son." The boy he motioned to follow him appeared to be about twelve years of age.

Using hooks, they hauled one of the overturned boats toward shore. Fifteen men of Darbenmore helped them haul in the boats they could reach, and then climb in those boats and go after the vessels that had drifted farther into the bay.

Otec locked gazes with Destin. "You and the rest of the men, help the Darbens bring in the boats."

He turned then to see Dobber set his mother gently down on the shore. The waves lapped hungrily at her feet, as if they had tasted her once and craved to do so again. Otec could see she was dying. Though he didn't want to, he moved toward his friend's side.

"All your life," his mother gasped, "you protected them. But when it mattered most, you left us. You ran. And my boys died."

Otec's mouth fell open. He should not be hearing this. He started slowly moving away.

Dobber shook his head. "They killed Father as if he was nothing. And then they looked at me, and I knew they would kill me too."

She turned away from him. "I'll be with my real sons soon. And you'll remain here, alone. Because that's what you chose when you abandoned us."

Otec felt a shell crunch under his feet. Dobber whipped around and their gazes locked. Dobber cried out. "Don't—don't tell anyone."

Otec could only nod.

His mother laughed. "He won't have to. You'll wear the mark of your shame for the rest of your life."

"Dobber, she's not thinking clearly. She's—"

But she only cackled and then her eyes shut. Her breathing grew increasingly labored, and then it stopped. The rising tide kept coming, stealing her back into its embrace.

"Dobber, I left too, when I probably should have stayed. It doesn't mean—"

Dobber rose to his feet, a growing darkness in his gaze. "Don't." He pushed past Otec without looking back.

16

It was agreed that Enrid and the other women would stay in Darbenmore until Otec sent word that it was safe for them to return to the Shyle. The remaining clanmen piled into ten boats, each carrying around fifteen men. Nineteen men from Darbenmore came with them, to work the single-square-sailed vessels and navigate the mystery of the ocean.

The men of Darben assured Otec that they could maneuver their vessels much faster than any Raider. The plan was to come upon the Raiders and flank them on both sides, then board the boats, kill the Raiders, and set the women free. No one discussed the fact that the Shyle men couldn't swim, but the knowledge hung over them like rot on a carcass.

Otec made sure Destin was in the boat with him—he didn't want the man sowing dissension. Otec also kept the Argon boys close; they mostly ate and slept, so it wasn't too hard to keep an eye on them.

Dobber chose a boat as far away from Otec as possible. It was probably better that way. Otec still couldn't look at him without thinking about how he'd abandoned his family.

From his position at the rudder, Halfed, the Darben man in Otec's boat, pointed to the dark smudge of clouds in the distance. "If they come this way, we'll have to beach the boats—they're not meant to handle a storm."

"Where?" Otec asked. They had been skimming past the abrupt cliffs all day, zigzagging back and forth to tack into the wind.

The man squinted at the cliff's base and didn't respond. But he kept dividing his attention between the clouds and the base of the cliffs.

"How long before we see the clan lands?" Destin asked again.

Halfed looked at the cliffs, then the sails. "Tomorrow, maybe. I've never gone this far."

Matka cut up the fish she'd managed to catch and handed it to the six men in their small fishing vessel. The rolling of the ocean seemed to have no effect on her. She pushed some fish into Otec's hands—it was raw as they had no way to cook it. "You should eat," she told him. "You're going to need your strength."

Wishing for something hot to ease the bone-deep cold of his hands, he grimaced and forced some of the fish down his throat. He watched her make her way to the back of the boat. He stood to follow her, carefully easing around the sleeping men, who had wedged up against the gunwales to get out of the wind. He made his way to Matka's side and washed his hands in the freezing water, then splashed his face, the salt stinging his eyes. "I swear, someday I'll find a way to make Idara pay for what they've done to you, to me, to my family," he said.

She hacked off a piece of the fish head, forced a hook through it, and tossed it overboard. "You will pay the highest price for your hatred." She chuckled bitterly. "I should know."

He looked at her, really looked at her. Her hair had grown some in the month since he'd known her, but it still looked like a boy's hair. And all Otec really knew was that she'd risked her life to save his, to save his clan, his family. "Who are you?"

A sad smile graced her face. "I am what I said. A highwoman, daughter of a slave."

Otec shook his head, not understanding. She closed her eyes as if overwhelmed. He stared at the gray ocean meeting the gray sky. Slavery. That was the future in store for his sisters.

Matka pierced a fish's eye on a hook and tossed it overboard. "When they realized my sister and I had the Sight," she said so softly he almost couldn't hear her words over the wind, "we were taken from our mother. Forbidden from speaking the language of our homeland. I only saw my mother once more before she died."

A tear strayed down Matka's cheek. She didn't bother wiping it away as she stabbed another piece of meat with a hook. "I made sure the man who murdered her paid for what he'd done."

One of the lines went taut. Matka wrapped some ripped cloth over her palms and hauled in the wriggling silver fish, then bashed it on the head with the blunt side of the knife. "That's how I know about hatred, about how it cankers your soul. Revenge does nothing to ease the pain, only twists you into something you come to hate."

She sliced through the fish, pulling out its guts and bones. "When I first came to the clan lands, I saw kindness and beauty and love. I didn't understand it at first—I felt like I was being used for a purpose I couldn't yet understand. But when I was in the mountains with you, I realized that's just how the clans are. I never wanted to leave. But I wasn't sure I could abandon my sister. Even if she and I don't get along."

"What made you change your mind?" Otec said softly.

"You," Matka answered without looking at him. "And Holla." Her voice broke. "When I realized Jore had lied to me—that I had unwittingly been a part of this war—I knew I couldn't let you die for it."

And Otec had cursed her for it. "And your sister?"

Matka finally wiped her eyes. "She's lost to me now. She'll think I'm dead. And if she learns different, it will only harm her."

Otec frowned. "Why?"

Matka laughed bitterly. "My sister doesn't remember much of the apathy of our father. Or the love of our mother. She remembers the temple of fire and the palace. Incense and idols. And she wants to be high priestess, the master of it all. As high priestess, she would be second only to the king."

"She can't see what Idara has done?" Otec thought the girl a fool, but he didn't want to hurt Matka.

"Idara will spread the religion of the Goddess around the world—Suka thinks it our duty."

Matka and Otec sat quietly for a time, chewing raw fish. "What did you promise them, Matka?" he said finally. Not wanting to upset her, he didn't use the word "fairies."

She rinsed her hands in the ocean. "Our firstborn daughter. Which is why you and I can never be, Otec. Because I would not curse my child with their dark attention. I would not force her into that kind of slavery."

Matka looked up at him, her eyes moist. "What did you promise her?" Not wanting to answer, he looked away. "Otec?" she prodded. "She wouldn't have talked to you unless she wanted something."

He sighed. "I promised to save you. In return, she helped me drive back the Raiders until help could arrive."

Matka grunted. "Save me so that I might live to bear you a daughter." She stared at the knife. "My story hurts—the telling of it. It's like cutting out pieces of myself and passing them around." She sniffed. "But you need to know me, Otec, all of it. So you understand why."

He thought then of the secret he carried—of Jore's death. Perhaps it was wrong to keep it from her. "Matka, Jore . . . he—"

"I don't want to know," she said firmly. She stabbed into the fish again, then cut and sliced and tore.

Otec watched her, knowing he had lost her before he'd ever had her. And with her gone, he was truly alone. He turned his face into the bitter wind coming off the ocean, his heart a coffin of ice and snow.

17

A hand shook Otec's shoulder. He looked up into Destin's face. The man nodded once and then went about waking the rest of the clanmen.

Rubbing his eyes, Otec sat up, noticing he was warm on the side of his body where Matka was wedged against him. He automatically scanned for the Argon boys and saw them huddled together for warmth.

He peered into the predawn sky, which was still more black than gray. "What? What is it?"

Halfed looked back at him. "I caught sight of the other ships before sunset."

"Why didn't you tell us?" Otec growled.

The man grunted. "Because none of you would have slept, and you all look as if you've been scraped from the bottom of a boat."

Otec held out his hand for Matka's telescope. He saw the boats and could make out individuals through the lens.

"We caught up to them," Destin said.

"Of course we did." Halfed sniffed. "They don't have the men of Darben to steer for them."

Otec's gaze snagged on lights beyond the boats. "What is that?"

Matka took the telescope from him and peered through. Her mouth hardened. "The Idaran Armada."

The Argon boys scrambled forward at that, trying to get a glimpse of the ships that were supposedly the size of a small mountain.

That meant they were back at the clan lands. Otec rose to his feet, looking toward the cliffs, which weren't as high as in Darben. "That's Reisen."

Matka swung the telescope toward the shore. "There are two distinct camps."

"So this is where the army is clashing?" Ivar asked.

She nodded.

The boat continued to gain on the Raiders. "When we get close enough, we'll hook their boats and you'll have to jump across," Halfed said.

Matka looked at the cliffs through her telescope as the clanmen shifted and pulled out their axes and shields.

"Make sure you don't hit any of our people," Otec said. He met Dobber's gaze in another of the boats, and the man looked quickly away.

The Idarans noticed them shortly thereafter. They were close enough now, and there was just enough light for Otec to distinguish his people from the Idarans. A Raider in one of the boats stood up. It was Tyleze. "You come near us," he shouted, "and we'll start killing them."

Otec stared at the Raiders in disbelief. He should have realized they would try this, should have planned better. But he'd never imagined men evil enough to kill unarmed women and children.

For the second time, Otec looked into his family members' eyes. Holla pointed wildly toward the shore. "There are Raiders on the cliffs!" A Raider on the boat jumped on her, but Aldi and

Wesson rammed the man in unison. "You have to warn them, Otec. You have to!" Holla shouted.

Otec shook his head. "I have to save you, Holla! I have to save all of you!"

"Otec," Matka said as she peered through her telescope. "She's right. There are Idarans scaling the cliffs."

"What?"

"Hundreds of them." She handed Otec the telescope so he could see for himself. "The camp is still asleep. If they attack now . . ."

"And the main army attacks from the east . . ." Destin trailed off.

"The effects would be devastating," Matka finished for him.

Slowly lowering the telescope, Otec gazed at his family. Tyleze held a knife to Holla's throat. "You decide, clanman. Do they live or die?"

Otec locked gazes with each of his siblings in turn, Storm last of all. She picked something up and gently pulled back the wrapping to reveal the face of a baby.

Otec was an uncle. He still didn't know if the child was a boy or a girl. "What would you have me do, Storm? You tell me, and I'll do it."

The Raiders made no move to stop her from speaking, but they drew their swords and stood over her. "It's too late for us, Otec. And if you don't stop them, there won't be a Shyle for any of you to go back to."

Her words shattered his frozen heart into a thousand pieces. "Storm . . ."

She gave him a gentle smile. "Sometimes you have to lose a sheep to save the flock," she said through her tears. The other women in the boat called out similar sentiments, begging the men to go.

From his own boat, Otec heard crying and turned to see tears streaming down Ivar's ruddy cheeks. Otec's gaze shifted to his fellow clanmen and came to rest on Destin. "What do we do?"

"Is it not better that the Raiders kill them now," Destin said, "rather than letting them live on as slaves?"

"No," Matka answered without looking up from the water speeding past the boat. "For their children will be free." She met Destin's gaze. "Besides, could you live with yourself if you were the reason they were murdered?"

He winced and then slowly shook his head. "No."

"I say we go after them," Dobber shouted from one of the other boats. Some of the other men roared their agreement. "We might be able to save some."

"Otec, you must decide now or it will be too late," Matka said.

"Lose a sheep. Save the herd," he murmured to himself. Suddenly, he realized he truly was the clan chief. Right now, he had to be a leader. Had to put the fate of entire clans before the fate of a few dozen individuals. Even if that decision tore out his heart and destroyed him.

He glanced up at each of his siblings in turn. "I'm sorry," he cried, falling to the deck and bruising his knees. "I'm sorry I wasn't fast enough."

"Be a good clan chief." Storm said through her sobs. "Make it better than it was."

"I will," Otec promised as he gripped the edge of the boat, hanging on as if his life depended on it.

Tyleze eased his knife away from Holla's throat. "I love you!" she cried. "Never forget!"

Tyleze hauled her to Storm and set her down, then ordered his crew to make for the armada. Otec stared at his sisters until the details of their faces were lost to the distance. Stared at them as they lost their distinct forms, becoming indistinguishable from one another. Stared until he lost them—his family.

Then he turned his back on his sisters, on the women of their village. "We need to figure out a way to alert the army. And we need to take out those Raiders."

18

Destin rested a hand on Otec's shoulder. "You did the right thing."

Otec could only nod.

"We can handle the Raiders," Ake said as he and his brother tugged out their bows.

"They'll make good target practice," Arvid agreed.

"I can use fire arrows to signal your clanmen," Matka said. "They'll see them and know something is wrong."

Otec grunted in approval. He turned to face the dozen boats following him. "Aim for the men you can hit. When you run out of arrows, use your slings."

As the cliffs came closer, he measured wind and distance. He'd never shot anything from a boat, but it couldn't be much different than a moving horse. He'd just fire at the top of the swell.

When they were within range, Otec cast one last glance in the direction his siblings had disappeared. And then he turned away, pulled back his bow, sighted along the shaft, and released. The other men in the boats did the same, dropping Raiders from the cliffs like spiders. But soon the clanmen ran out of arrows.

Halfed ran the boats aground. Otec used the momentum in his leap, landing in the water with a splash that soaked his heavy boots. He sloshed to shore and snatched up handfuls of rocks. He took out his sling and let stone after stone fly—he was a pretty good shot, as one never ran out of stones in the Shyle.

Matka crouched down to gather driftwood. Then she dumped it into a pile and attacked it with sparks from her flint and striker. The moment she had a flame going, she wrapped her five reserved arrows in shredded bark and tied it off in a messy knot. She pulled a small pouch from her pocket and sprinkled the powder over the bark. "If this is the last time I'll ever see your flames, Goddess, let them burn bright."

Matka drew back her bow and sent the arrow up over the rim of the cliff, the flames trailing behind like a multicolored comet. "I'd like to see your clanmen miss that," she said.

When the clanmen saw the arrows, they'd know someone was down on the beach. They would come to investigate and would find the Raiders trying to sneak up on them.

She sent off five arrows in all, directing them over the cliff to burn where all could see. The Idarans on the cliffs began to panic. Those closer to the top continued climbing up. Those nearer the bottom started back down.

Otec and his men continued to send stones at them until the Raiders at the base of the cliffs began firing arrows back. He hauled Matka behind him and held out his shield. An arrow thudded into it, piercing through. Otec almost ordered the boys to go in the boats and stay out of range, but then he remembered what it felt like to be left behind and kept his mouth shut.

"Nice of them to share," Destin said with a crazed grin as he began picking off the arrows and firing them back.

Otec surveyed the growing gathering of Raiders at the base of the cliffs and knew he had to charge them and wipe them out before his men were outnumbered. "Axes!" he called out.

The clanmen put away their slings and hauled out their axes. This time he did meet the boys' gazes. "Stay back," Otec ordered. "Honor to the Shyle!" he cried as they charged.

Sprinting across the rocky beach, Otec sidestepped a thrust and chopped through a Raider's block to land the axe in his face. He stepped past the man to meet the next. Matka danced beside him, keeping his left flank secure, while Destin took up his right. Otec blocked a swipe of one sword, stomped on the low-swinging second blade, and head-butted the Idaran, who staggered back. Otec kicked him down and buried his axe in the man's chest.

A cry came from Otec's right and he turned to see Destin staggering back, blood gushing from his leg. Otec took a step to help him, but Matka was there first. Gritting his teeth, Otec gave ground. "Tighten up!" A Raider's sword slipped through his shield, piercing his arm and making it go numb. His blood made the grip slippery.

Another sword pierced his legs. With a roar, he ducked behind his shield and charged, knocking over three men. Matka and Destin finished them off. Otec kicked one in the temple and chopped at the other two.

A man fell screaming from the cliffs, landing on the Raider who was fighting Otec. Now both Raiders lay still and broken. Otec glanced up to see Raiders being thrown or shoved off the cliffs. "Retreat!" he cried to his men, having no desire to be crushed.

He ran over the rocky shore, his boots soggy and his arm numb. When he turned back, his clanmen were cheering from the tops of the cliffs. The men of the Shyle charged back in quickly dispatched any remaining Raiders.

When the last of them were taken care of, Otec turned to Matka. "Do you trust me?"

She turned to see the clanmen tossing down long ropes. He grabbed one and made to tie it around her waist so they could haul her up. "Oh, no," she said, face going ashen. "Not again."

He took hold of her hand. "Come on. I promise I won't let you fall."

19

Arms trembling, Otec hauled himself over the cliff and turned to heave Matka up. She staggered a couple steps and then lay face-down on the ground, arms spread as if hugging the rocks.

He watched to make sure their six injured were hauled up safely. He shook out his numb and burning hands and searched the faces around him, his eyes watering at the brisk wind. The Reisen clan chief, Gen, marched up to them, bloody axe in hand. "Where's Hargar?"

Otec's jaw tightened at the mention of his father. "I'm Clan Chief Otec, his oldest living son."

For a moment, Gen seemed incapable of speaking, but then he muttered under his breath, "Cursed Raiders." He seemed to shake himself as he looked over their ragged band. "Can you fight?"

Otec didn't have to ask his men to know their answer. "After some rest and food, yes. I've six injured who need to be cared for." He figured most of them would live.

Gen nodded. "I can give you food, and an easy assignment for rest. The Cors and what few Argons we have are holding the front lines, but we need to spell them."

Matka gasped. "Wait!" She pushed herself to her feet. "The Idarans will have something else planned. They always do."

Gen looked her over like she was a beetle in one of his barrels of rye. "You're one of them."

Otec moved in front of her, and the Argon boys immediately stepped up next to him. "She was their slave," Otec said firmly. "Without her help, the Shyle would be gone, and possibly the whole of the clan lands as well."

Gen motioned to his men. "Tie her up. I don't want her signaling the rest of them."

Destin stepped up beside the Argon boys. "I suppose you don't need the Shyle's help after all."

Otec shot Destin an appreciative glance and noticed the rest of his men had tightened up and were staring Gen down.

"Fine," Gen growled. "But she's not fighting with us. We've killed enough Raiders posing as highmen—we'd hardly notice one more." He took a step back and pointed to a tent. "There's food and water there. Take what you need. Quickly."

The Shyle clanmen bunched around Otec, forming a phalanx of protection around Matka. He strode toward the tent, nearly a hundred of his men around him.

"And Otec," Gen called out. Otec looked back. "Make sure she stays there."

Otec didn't respond. They filed through the tent door. It was a relief to be out of the wind, even if it was steamy inside the tent. There was rye gruel, beer, and boiled vegetables. He took a huge helping of each, sat on the ground, and bolted the food down before he could taste any of it.

Matka sat beside him, but instead of eating, she tended to his wounds. "Matka . . ." he began.

"It's all right. I saw a tent for the wounded, and I'd rather be there, healing instead of injuring. I'll make sure your clanmen are looked after."

Otec shifted uncomfortably on the rocky ground. "I don't like it."

She tipped her head to look up at him. "They'd be fools to trust me." She reached into her pack and handed him her telescope. "Find the high ground and keep your eyes open."

"Matka, could you go after them?" he asked carefully.

"I've thought about it," she whispered. "I am known to many people in Idara. If I go back, it will be to my death. But if you ask it of me, I will."

Otec closed his eyes. "No." There was no use, not if she would die.

Gen appeared at the tent flap. "Shyle, time to go."

Otec pushed to his feet. The ground seemed to pitch under him as he struggled to stave off a wave of exhaustion. "Don't do anything foolish."

Matka rolled her eyes. "I'm not the one marching into battle."

Yes, but she was surrounded by people who thought she was the enemy. He reached back and squeezed her hand before striding outside. It was nearly dawn now. Light enough to see the heated battle in the middle of a field of crushed grain.

As Otec walked with him through the tents, Gen explained, "My men and I will push to the front—the Raiders have been concentrating on punching through our middle—and the Argons and Cors will gradually fall back as we replace them.

"I'll post you there, on that high ground." Gen pointed to a steep hill topped by a tumbling of rocks and boulders surrounded by a stretch of trees, the foliage the rusty red of old blood. "Those men have been up there since midday yesterday. The Raiders have been foolish enough to rush it a few times. But they're easily repelled with slings and bows."

Otec agreed, grateful his men wouldn't be thrown right into the thick of battle. He gestured for them to follow and started up the incline.

Gen reached out, taking hold of Otec's arm. "If you lose that hill, our whole north flank will be exposed."

Otec nodded and Gen let him go. Otec climbed the rocky ground. In the forest, he noticed the trees had crusty boils across their surface—some type of blight, perhaps. He walked on the corpses of the diseased leaves, feeling blisters starting in his wet boots.

He and his men crossed behind the Reisen holding the front, until they reached the knobby hill, its twin on the other side of a field of rye. The Reisen greeted them gratefully, showed them where the artillery was, and departed with heavy steps.

Otec surveyed the area, which was covered in a scattering of boulders, most just big enough to provide cover for a man to lie behind. They would make it easily defendable.

While the men of the Shyle spread out among the rocks and boulders, getting comfortable and wringing saltwater from their boots, Otec braced himself against the wind on a boulder just taller than a man and perched precariously on two smaller boulders. He pulled out Matka's telescope. Nervous after her warning, he searched the forest along the sides of the hill, and below that, the field of golden rye that should have long since been harvested. It had already dropped much of the grain. And it was dropping more, leaving the precious food on the ground to rot.

Otec stared at the stalks, which were taller than a man. Something was wrong. They should be shifting with the wind in wave-like patterns. But this looked more like a hail of pebbles scattered across the still surface of a pond.

"Destin!" he called. The man looked up from where he was wringing saltwater from the felt liner of his boots. "Come here!"

Destin shoved his feet in and pushed over to Otec's side, taking the telescope from his hands. "I don't see anything."

"The rye—it's moving wrong." Matka's warning pounding against his memory, Otec took the telescope and rested his gaze on the sickly trees. It was eerily quiet. "And the forest."

"I don't see anything there either," Destin said.

"That's what's wrong. There should at least be birds flitting about." Otec lowered the telescope. "Send the twins after the men who just left. I want them back here. And send Ivar to the Reisen down the line. We're surrounded on two sides and we need reinforcements."

"Gen said his men easily repelled their attack before." Destin took a step closer. "They won't pull men from the front lines, not when they're under heavy attack."

Otec's gaze shifted between the trees and the rye, thinking of the cliffs he'd just climbed. "The plan was to position men at our flanks, making our front lines bulge forward. They'll surround us, cut us off, and finish this."

It was brilliant. And it would work if he didn't move fast. Destin was already backing away. "Otec, are you sure?"

He didn't bother answering but dropped from the boulder, his blisters popping and fluid oozing around his heels. He grabbed the Argon boy's shoulders and gave orders himself.

Then he moved among his men, saying, "Take defensive positions among these rocks, and set yourself up with arrows and stones. But don't hurry. We don't want to push them into attacking us yet—we'll be overrun if they do."

Finally, Destin nodded and started gathering up more men. And then they waited.

Ivar came back first. "Gen says to calm down. A hundred men have held this hill for a week."

Otec ground his teeth. "That's because the Raiders let him hold this hill."

The twins came back again, a hundred grumbling Reisen trailing behind them. A grizzled man took hold of Otec's shirt. "Listen, boy, you might be a clan chief, but my axe has killed more Raiders than—"

Otec shoved him away. "Your men will move into position around these rocks. And you will do it now!"

The man stepped back, glaring at him. "We haven't eaten since midday last."

"Now," Otec said as he eased his axe from his belt.

The man looked at the axe, then back at Otec. The man at his side took hold of his arm. "Ymir, he outranks you."

Ymir shook him off. "Gen will have you to the beating pole for this, clan chief or not."

Otec stared him down, and Ymir motioned to the hundred Reisen behind him. "Back into position. This fool Shyle—"

His rant was interrupted by Destin shouting, "Raiders!"

Otec shoved his axe back in place and climbed back on the tallest boulder, then took hold of his bow and started firing at the men rushing out of the field in such numbers they shook the remaining seeds from the stalks. He didn't even need to aim for the sheer number of them; he simply fired three arrows at once into the front line, then took hold of three more and fired again.

Two hundred men firing arrows on two sides left a line of dead the Raiders had to clamber over. And still they kept coming.

"They're attacking the Reisen at the base of the hill!" cried one of Otec's men.

Otec swung his bow around, taking out men as they cleared the trees. If they could punch behind the Reisens' lines, they would have the hill surrounded. "We have to hold this hill!" Otec yelled as Raiders fell with the blighted leaves.

For a while, his men held the Raiders back, killing them faster than they could climb. But they just kept coming—hundreds upon hundreds of them. And Otec's men were running out of arrows. The men moved seamlessly to slings, flinging stones nearly as quickly as the arrows had flown. Otec joined them, taking stones from a stack someone had already set up on top of the boulder. Soon the stacks of stones had dwindled down to bare rock. Men scrambled along the ground, slinging anything they could find.

The Raiders crested their wave of dead and began advancing up the hill.

"We have to retreat," Dobber called out from Otec's right.

"If we lose this hill, we lose the only advantage the north flank has," Otec replied. He found the twins and motioned them toward the main camp. "We need arrows. And order any men in the camp up here now!"

The boys took off at a dead run. Otec turned back to the battle just as the first Raider crested the hill, his swords thrusting forward. Destin chopped down on the folded steel, shoved the man back with his shield, and swung his axe down.

This was repeated across the lines by the handful. But without enough men keeping the Raiders at bay with their slings, another dozen snuck in. And another. Dobber was in trouble, two men fighting him at once.

Otec hooked his sling on his belt and took his shield in hand. He dropped down from his boulder, axe swinging. The Raider was dead before he fell. Otec swung at the Raider fighting Dobber, cutting into his legs. Dobber finished him with a strong swing.

Otec whirled around. He blocked and chopped, his arms past feeling. Swords sliced past his shield. Dozens of cuts crisscrossed his skin. Yet his men held.

Destin appeared on his right. "They just keep coming."

"Gen has to see our need," Otec panted, his axe seeming heavier and heavier. "He has to send reinforcements." But the men came only from the direction of the encampment. And they were going to be too late.

Sweat ran down Dobber's face. "Otec," he gasped, "if we don't retreat now, we're all going to die."

"If we retreat" —Otec used the backswing of his axe to bash in a Raider who'd tried to sneak up behind him— "the Raiders will overrun us all."

A cry came from his right and he turned to see Dobber staggering back, blood gushing from his leg. Otec took a step to help him, but Destin was suddenly there, driving the edge of his shield into the man's back and saving Dobber's life.

But the move left Destin open to the man he'd been fighting, and the Raider took advantage, shoving his sword into Destin's back. The Raider leapt over Destin's falling body and rushed at Dobber.

Otec rammed the Raider with the lips of his shield, swept his legs out from under him, and killed him with one downward swing. He whipped around to find Destin in his death throes. Dobber gaped at the dying man and began backing away, his head shaking vehemently. "No, no, no, no, no!"

"Dobber—" Otec sidestepped a thrust, sweeping the Raider's swords to the side with his shield, and following it up with a quick chop. He looked over his shoulder to see Dobber running, leaving Otec's right flank open. "Dobber!" he shouted as two men at once descended on him.

Gritting his teeth, Otec gave ground. "Tighten up!" A Raider's sword slipped through his shield, piercing his already wounded arm.

Another sword pierced his leg. He was losing too much blood. And his reactions were growing slower. Otec backed up, knowing he needed help. A swing came, and he knew he would be too slow to block.

20

The Raider froze mid-swing, eyes bulging. By the hundreds, arrows rained down on the Raiders swarming the hill. But the arrows came from behind the Raiders.

Otec staggered back and his clanmen stepped forward, blocking him from the Raiders. He let his arms fall, his axe and shield too heavy to hold up anymore. He traced the path of the arrows back to the hill on the other side of the rye field. He lifted his telescope and stared through it at a company of Argons. "Where did they . . ." and then he saw Seneth shouting out orders to what had to be two hundred and fifty men. "By the Balance, he's got at least a hundred boys with him."

Otec heard a thunk and turned to see his axe had slipped from his hands. He stared at it, wondering how it had gotten on the ground. And then he saw the blood running like a river down his arm. He staggered back and realized his boots were full of blood. He fell to his knees and turned to see men from the encampment cresting the hill on the south side, Matka leading them.

He reached for her, but the movement threw him off balance. He tipped over, landing hard on the rocks. Otec stared at the sky, wondering if this was how the leaves felt as they died, their colors bleeding out.

And then Matka blocked his view. She didn't say a word, just opened a bag and tied a ripped rag tight on his upper arm.

Another woman knelt beside her. Otec recognized her—Ressa, Gen's wife. "This is Otec? Should we move him?"

"No!" Matka said breathlessly. "If I don't get his bleeding stopped, he'll be dead before we get anywhere."

Ressa glanced around. "But we're at the front lines."

Matka leaned over Otec, looking into his eyes. "I've been on the front lines all my life." Her words whispered against his lips. "Stay with me, Otec, and I'll give you anything you want."

He looked into her dark eyes, determination rising like a wave within him. "Stay."

Tears pooling in her eyes, she nodded. "All right. I'll stay if you will."

He smiled then, for he knew he'd won.

21

I t took two months and a harsh winter to finally drive the Raiders from the clan lands' shores. Braving the freezing wind off the ocean, Otec found Matka standing well back from the edge of the cliffs, watching the departing Raider ships.

His gaze dropped to the item she was rubbing her thumb across. She held the elice blossom he had carved for her. The stem had long ago broken off, and he noticed the wood was shiny from the oils of her hands.

So she had held the carving and rubbed it often. The thought made Otec bold. Fighting the dizziness that plagued him whenever he moved, he stood beside her, looking out over the water.

"They'll be back," Matka said without looking at him. "Defeating them though they outnumbered you two to one . . . King Kutik's humiliation will turn to hatred. And they will be back."

"Then we'll defeat them again." Otec stared at the ships, wondering if his sisters and younger brothers were aboard any of them, or already on their way to Idara.

With enormous effort, he pushed the thought out of his mind and said, "I've spoken with Seneth—he's agreed to marry us."

Matka turned to look at Otec. "I didn't promise to marry you."

He realized he should have been more specific, but then he had been dying at the time. "I know you love me."

She wet her lips. "You know I can't."

He touched her face—he'd been longing to touch her like this ever since the waterfall. "I won't live my life in fear of curses. I see what I want. And I'm going to take it."

"I can't do that to our daughter."

Otec stepped closer to her, unable to stand the distance between them. "Who says we'll even have a daughter? All our children could be boys. Or we could die tomorrow and have no children at all. All I know is that we have to seize what happiness we can while we can."

Matka closed her eyes as if the thought were physically painful. "Otec . . ."

Her hair had grown nearly to her chin. She was kind and good and strong. Most importantly, she held Otec's heart, and he held hers. "No," he said. Her head came up as he stepped closer again. "You are my light," he continued. "Without you, the darkness would swallow me whole. I will not give you up. I will not allow anything else to be taken from me."

She stared into his gaze with watering eyes. "But the fairies are tricksy and cruel."

He tucked a lock of hair behind her ears. "And we are strong and brave."

Matka gave a sad smile. "I wish you could be that innocent man again. That the darkness had let you be."

Otec took her face in his hands. "But then I would never have appreciated the light. Marry me?"

She tipped her head back, the sunlight touching her cheeks. A smile spread across her mouth. "I will."

Otec kissed her warm lips—lips that tasted of sunshine.

EPILOGUE

With the cool spring breeze blowing across his back, Otec finished hammering the last shingle on the clan house's new roof. He took a moment to look around his village. Most of the homes that could be saved were nearly finished. The rest were being knocked down, the salvageable stones to be reused in building new houses. Still, the village was only about half the size it had been, and the number of burial mounds behind the clan house had nearly doubled.

The dirt was still fresh, the mounds an open wound on the face of the land. None of the graves held Otec's loved ones; the right of burying them had been stolen from him too. Over time, grass and flowers would grow over them. The dirt would compact. But the graves would never completely fade.

As his eyes strayed to Shyle Pass, he thought of his sisters. Storm's baby would be crawling by now. He wondered if it was a boy or a girl. If his sisters had survived. If Holla's spirit had been broken. How he could possibly be happy when they were slaves.

Otec tried to push such dark thoughts away, but it was not easy. So he did what he always did when the darkness threatened to cripple him—he went looking for Matka.

He found her in the barn, covered in hay and blood. She was smiling as she cleared the birth sack from the lamb's face. "She came out backwards, but I managed to save her."

Through the darkness that haunted him, Matka had become his light. When the night came and neither of them could sleep, they held each other, the child growing in her belly a wonderful, terrifying lump between them.

She went to the bucket of rainwater and washed her arms, chatting about the ewes and the new lambs—gifts from the other clans. She sobered when she told Otec that Dobber was so deep in the drink he had accidentally gone to the Bends' home last night instead of his own. They couldn't wake him to get him out, so he'd ended up sleeping on their floor.

As Matka chattered on, Otec felt a swelling within him, a lightness that threatened to burst. And then she suddenly went silent, her hands going to her enormous belly. He stepped toward her, arms out to catch her if she fell. "Matka?"

She grimaced and tried to cover it up with a smile. But her face was dark red, and she was holding her breath. She gripped his hand and hunched over.

"Has your time come?" When she still didn't answer, he wrapped an arm around her and helped her to the clan house. "How long have the pains been coming?" Otec knew more than most men about birth—after all, his mother and sisters had brought most of the Shyle's babies into the world.

Matka let out a long breath. "All morning. I thought they might go away like the others."

He set her down in the kitchen and hurried up the ladder to fetch blankets and pillows. "I'm getting Enrid."

"No, I—" Matka's voice cut off. She pinched her eyes shut and nodded.

Otec sprinted through the village and shoved open the door to Enrid's house. She took one look at him and simply grabbed her bag.

Not waiting for her, he ran back to the clan house. Matka had squatted in front of the empty hearth, both hands resting on the rock fireplace. He crouched beside her. "What do you want me to do?"

Enrid stepped through the doorway. "Get outside with you. This is woman's work." Otec looked at Matka, his eyes begging her to let him stay. Enrid rolled her eyes. "You won't want him here, Matka."

Matka nodded for him to go.

Jaw clenched, he paced outside the kitchen door, wearing a pathway through the weeds. When his wife let out her first moan, he stopped and dropped down by the door. For the first time in a long time, he wanted to carve something, take all his nervous energy and create something beautiful with it.

While Matka moaned and panted, Otec went in search of a piece of wood. His knife sawed through the rough exterior, cutting away until he reached bright, virgin wood. He sliced away one layer at a time, leaving beautiful whorls that piled up around him. Once he had the basic shape, he added details—the legs, the ears, the tail—until he had a magnificent stallion, ears perked, face proud. He wished he had the paint to make it black, with a star on his forehead, for that's what he envisioned.

A wail rose up from inside the house—an infant's cry. Otec's eyes welled with tears at such a familiar sound, one that had been severely lacking from a home that used to echo with the cries of children.

He stepped inside to see Matka holding their child and staring at a scrunched-up red face below a tuft of wild blond hair. Tears streamed down Matka's cheeks as she smiled brightly up at Otec.

Enrid stepped past him. "I'll be back in a moment."

Barely hearing her depart, he dropped to his knees and unwrapped the blanket a little. A grin broke across his face. He wrapped the child again and touched his forehead to Matka's. "You see. I told you they could not control us."

She chuckled, opening her mouth to respond, when a flurry of wings made Otec's head jerk up. The owl fairy flew into the room in her human-like form, gazing at his child. Otec put himself between them—he didn't even want the creature to look upon his baby.

"I see you have your son," the fairy said smoothly.

He took his carving knife in hand, wishing it was his axe. "Yes, a son. Not a daughter."

She tipped her head. "Foolish human. I do not set the board, only the players. Your son is important to the game—just not as important as his sister will be."

Otec launched the knife, but the fairy spun, wings whirling. She landed in a crouch on the kitchen table, her eyes glittering with rage.

He pointed to the door. "Get out and never come back. Or I will kill him myself and destroy your games once and for all."

She bared her teeth at him. "Liar."

Otec turned and took hold of his son. Matka held on, her expression fierce. He met her gaze, his eyes asking her to trust him.

She reluctantly released their baby. Otec took his son, love swelling within him as the boy blinked up at him. Otec held him over a bowl of water, hoping his face didn't betray the lie. "I'll drown him."

The fairy stepped back, her talons scraping against the table. "Enjoy your happiness, little human. Enjoy it while it lasts."

She flared her wings, shot through the open door, and disappeared from view. Otec sagged, holding his son to his chest. Matka sobbed behind him.

He crouched next to her and deposited his son in his wife's arms. "Only an infant, and he freed us from her presence."

"But what she said . . ."

Otec kissed her forehead. "She said we would have a daughter, and we had a son. She can't know the future—no one can."

Enrid barreled into the room. "Was that an owl?"

Otec ignored the midwife. "What will we call him?"

"Bratton," Matka said at once.

Otec pushed back her shoulder-length hair. "Why Bratton?"

She shrugged. "Because I like the way it sounds."

Otec had wanted to name him Hargar, after his father. But Matka's eyes were haunted, the bright joy of before overcome with shadows. He could give her this. "I like it," he said.

She took his hand. "Do you really think we can beat them?"

He rested his hand on his son's forehead. "We already have."

Amber Argyle is the number-one bestselling author of the Witch Song Series and the Fairy Queen Series. Her books have been nominated for and won awards in addition to being translated into French and Indonesian.

Amber graduated cum laude from Utah State University with a degree in English and physical education, a husband, and a two-year old. Since then, she and her husband have added two more children, which they are actively trying to transform from crazy small people into less crazy larger people.

To receive Amber Argyle's starter library for free,
simply tell her where to send it:
http://eepurl.com/l8fl1

OTHER TITLES BY AMBER ARGYLE

Witch Song Series

Witch Song
Witch Born
Witch Rising
Witch Fall

Fairy Queens Series

Of Ice and Snow
Winter Queen
Of Fire and Ash
Summer Queen
Of Sand and Storm
Daughter of Winter
Winter's Heir

CPSIA information can be obtained
at www.ICGtesting.com
Printed in the USA
BVOW10s1205141117
500389BV00018B/998/P